W9-DEY-660

The Secret Laboratory Journals of Dr. Victor Frankenstein

The Alchemical Homunculus.

The Secret Laboratory Journals of Dr. Victor Frankenstein

By: Jeremy Kay

THE OVERLOOK PRESS

WOODSTOCK • NEW YORK

First published in 1995 by
The Overlook Press
Lewis Hollow Road
Woodstock, New York   12498

Library of Congress Cataloging-in-Publication Data

Kay, Jeremy
The secret laboratory journal of Dr. Victor Frankenstein / Jeremy Kay.
p. cm.
1. Frankenstein (Fictitious character)—Fiction. 2. Monsters—Fiction. I. Title.
PS3561.A8837S4   1995
813'.54—dc20
93-25784   CIP

ISBN: 0-87951-511-2
Manufactured in the United States of America
Typeset by AeroType, Inc.

First Edition

Contents

PART I
The Beginnings
The Early Life of Victor Frankenstein, His Friends,
Family and Education
11

PART II
The Laboratory
Frankenstein's Discovery of His Family's Ancestral Castle
and His Preparations for the Great Work
45

PART III
Equipment and Materials
Acquisition and Construction of Laboratory Apparatus
65

PART IV
The Creature
Frankenstein's Human Life Rejuvenation Experiments
89

PART V
The Bride
Frankenstein Creates the Creature's Mate
133

PART VI
The Return
Frankenstein's Fate
151

INTRODUCTION

Mary Shelley's monster is a powerful image, brought to life not only by her genius doctor, but also by the countless Hollywood movies which have recreated this ill-fated creature, giving it shape and form, making it familiar around the world.

My first association with the Frankenstein mythos began as a school boy, scared witless in a darkened movie theater. Those shadowy black and white images of Boris Karloff, Elsa Lanchester and Colin Clive, accompanied by Franz Waxman's fearsome musical score, still call to mind monstrous memories. I then discovered the dark, smudged drawings from the *Classics Illustrated* comic book adaptation of the *Frankenstein* novel; and later still, the literary source of these powerful images - Mary Shelley's horrifying yet spellbinding Gothic novel, from which Frankenstein originated.

During this period of my childhood, American life was darkened by the frightening specter of Communism and the nascent nuclear age. The cold war affected all of post-war life, including its art, literature and popular culture. The bomb was the Frankenstein of our time— monstrous, capable of good and evil, created by scientists playing God.

That shadow has lifted somewhat, but as we approach the millennium, we have various genetic and biological experiments, conducted both publicly and privately, to remind us of the risks of human hubris.

Mary Wollstonecraft Shelley was 16 when she wrote *Frankenstein* and it was published "Anonymously" a year later in 1818. Her novel became an instant bestseller but, the publishers were unable to understand its popularity and were reluctant to reprint. Despite this *Frankenstein* became the most popular novel of its time and was followed the next year by a successful but controversial London stage play. That was, of course, only the beginning.

—JEREMY KAY

Santa Monica, 1994

What if, in an old trunk of stained black oak and trimmed in brass, now tarnished, one found an old journal among such effluvia as neatly-tied bundles of tattered letters, a cigar box filled with hundreds of fancy buttons of shell, bone and celluloid, and dozens of old magazines and books that crumble to the touch? What if, when one lifted the journal from the jumble of forgotten keepsakes, one could just make out, on the nearly disintegrated cover, the words, "Laboratory Journals of Dr. Victor Frankenstein?"

One's heart would stop.

What if upon opening the journal, gently and slowly to protect the ancient pages from damage, one found what appeared to be the notes of a scientist or doctor, well-versed not only in the accepted medical technology of the day and up-to-date in his knowledge of the newest experiments with electricity, but also masterfully educated in alchemy and the dark arts? What if the notes, sometimes meticulous, sometimes feverish, indicated that the author had usurped the divine power of bringing the dead back to life . . . and had succeeded?

What if Mary Shelley's Dr. Frankenstein was not a fictional character at all but based on a nineteenth century scientist whose secret work was the topic of whispered half-truths that circulated among the drawing rooms of the intelligentsia of the day?

What if the volume you are holding in your hands contains the journals of the historical Dr. Frankenstein and the illustrations that accompanied them, along with the finder's annotations on the material, with literary and artistic liberties taken to flesh out the story and to clarify some of the material?

What if a mortal being transgressed the limits of human knowledge?

I

The Beginnings

The Early Life of Victor Frankenstein,
His Friends, Family and Education

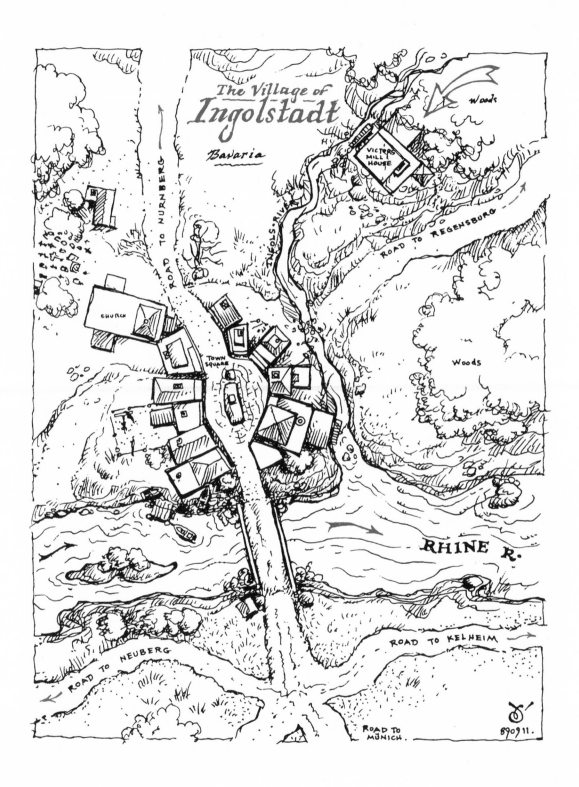

March, 1808.

I was born on August 4, 1792, in Switzerland. My family possessed a House on the outskirts of Geneva, a pleasant lake-front property where I grew to adolescence. As a Child I had all the pleasant amenities of the gentry, being attended by a faithful Nurse and Nanny, a Tutor and loving Parents.

Always fascinated by Nature, as a Boy, I would return to my Nursery with Pockets full of Frogs and Insects, only to be quietly admonished by my Nanny. My Tutor always complied with my wishes to discuss these fruits of Our Creator's labors, though his focus was more spiritual than secular.

By my seventh birthday (in 1799) I fully believed I knew all that was necessary to live in the World. Thus it was that I set out to visit the City of Geneva, where I had been on many occasions with my Father as he conducted his business. The path was familiar, so fearlessly I walked along without a care on that warm Summer's day.

Ancient Medicine

Ancient Greek theories of medicine, from as long ago as 600 B.C., prevailed in Europe in medieval times and well into the nineteenth century. These included the diagonistic techniques of examining the color of a patient's urine and the practice of bloodletting, or leeching. Underlying these and other medical procedures was the pervasive concept of the Four Humors, or fluidism. All matter was believed to be made up of the Four Elements—Fire, Water, Air, and Earth. Correspondingly, man, the microcosm, was also composed of four elements, or humors: Blood (Fire), Black Bile (Water), Yellow Bile (Air), and Phlegm (Earth). It was believed that when these humors were properly proportioned, health prevailed; if their balance was upset, sickness followed.

The ancient doctors also believed that each person possessed a single dominant humor, which determined his physical and emotional characteristics or temperament.

This theory prevailed unchallenged until 1858. With the publication of Rudolph Virchow's *Cellular Pathology*, an understanding of the function of cells finally replaced fluidism.

Not long after passing through the Gates of the City's Wall, I was circled by Crowds in the street. When I last came to town with Father the streets did not teem with people as they did on this day. Then, suddenly, I was jostled, bumped and cast to the ground. My Pocket was torn open and my three Coppers snatched by some unseen hand. My grand adventure had been cut short, and I became Concerned as late afternoon bowed to early evening.

When the Swiss Guards made ready to shut and lock the City Gates, my concern grew to despair. My predicament caused me to cry. One of the Swiss Soldiers approached and asked me to identify myself and tell from whence I came. I blurted out my whole Tale, including some indistinguishable mutterings of Father's business associate, M. Clerval, a local Merchant of some repute.

The Soldier then led me through Geneva's darkening cobbled Streets to the place of M. Clerval's Home and Business.

The Maid came to the Door, then led us upstairs to the withdrawing room, where I sat and the Soldier remained at attention, while we waited for M. Clerval.

The Scientific Method

By the dawn of the Industrial Revolution in England, (the 1820s to the 1840s), considerable advancements had been made in technological and mechanical sciences, and the art of medicine also benefited from this new and practical thinking. A logical system of analysis called the scientific method was developed. Better scientific results were produced as scientists began to (1) examine their evidence, (2) question the results, (3) arrive at logical conclusions, and (4) publish their findings for other scientists to learn from and apply in their own work.

The Theory of Life

The ancient quest for the "secret of life" was alluded to in Greek mythologies of Prometheus and Pygmalion and the Hebrew legends of the Golem, and later by the early alchemists, such as Paracelsus, Agrippa, Albertus Magnus, the Oriental Templars, and the Freemasons. They each attempted to create life through an alchemical distillation of various substances. This process reduced their base material into its most elementary essence, or "spirit," which was often depicted as a living miniature human, a Homunculus, formed within a glass laboratory alembic.

During this time, mechanical devices, wind-up artifacts, automata, and other cunning engines driven by the power of steam piqued the inventive imaginations of scientists and engineers. Despite all the progress made during this wondrous explosion of scientific advancement, the blasphemies of science were perceived as "acts against Heaven" and were therefore scorned by the pulpit. Civil laws were enacted to prevent further atrocities against the church, forcing scientific practices deeper underground.

In what seemed a long while, though was probably only a few minutes, Henry Clerval Sr., entered the Room.   His look was one of bewilderment, but as the Soldier explained the events, Clerval's mouth turned up in a pleasant smile. He instructed the Soldier to send word to my Father that I was safe and would be returned tomorrow.

Dismissing the Guard, Clerval then asked if I'd had my Dinner. When I replied that I had not, he opened the doors to his Family Dining Room and amidst a gathering of a dozen assorted Guests, I was seated while a Servant set another place.

It was on this night that I first met Henry Clerval (the Junior) and Elizabeth Lavenza, whom I later discovered was my near-distant Cousin. Both Children were about six years old, slightly younger than I. I could not anticipate then how intertwined our three lives would become.

From that time on as we grew older, Henry, Elizabeth and I became inseparable. We spoke about myriad Subjects, but were most pre-occupied with the Mysterious Powers of Nature. It was a foregone decision that I would study to become a Physician. Henry, it was assumed, would continue with his family's business, while Elizabeth would

The Beginnings of Electricity

During the late seventeenth and early eighteenth centuries, development of electrical processes accelerated. In 1675, a French astronomer, M. Jean Picard, was working with a barometer one night when he noticed it began to glow. This event caused great excitement, and Picard christened it the "Glow of Life."

By 1706, a student of Sir Isaac Newton's, Francis Hauksbee, constructed his "influence machine," a vacuum-filled glass globe which while spinning emitted a similar glow. He believed the cause to be friction. Over the next several years electrical knowledge progressed.

In the years that followed, electricity piqued the interest of the population throughout Europe. Its uses, not yet fully understood, were exhibited by traveling medicine shows and lecturers with wagonloads of equipment who moved from town to town, amazing crowds eager to know more about the "miracles of electricity."

simply have to marry us both, as we were both in love with her.

Knowing of my professional Desires, my Family generously allowed me to indulge in whatever books and publications which I believed to be useful. The more I read, the more I knew it was not mere Medicine which would fulfill my Scientific cravings. All my passion and all my enquiries were directed toward the Metaphysical.

This Natural Philosophy was the Genius which dictated my fate. I chanced to discover the Works of Cornelius Agrippa, Paracelsus and Albertus Magnus, carefully outlining the details of their methods.

I entered with the greatest diligence into the Search for the elusive Elixir of Life; the latter soon consumed my attention. If by some proper Chemical Process I could develop this Elixir, it would surely provide Mankind with limitless Knowledge and the Medicine to cure all ills.

I became impassioned with the raising of Ghosts and Devils, a notion which had been assigned to me by my then favorite Authors; the fulfillment of which I most eagerly sought. If my Incantations were not always successful, I attributed my failure to inexperience and mistaken procedures.

In the 1730s, James Graham's London Temple of Health displayed a bizarre attraction, the Celestial or Magnetico-Electrico Bed, on which childless couples would indulge in reproductive activities under a "therapeutic blanket of electricity."

By 1745, von Kleist had "stored" electricity in glass jars, which he named after the University of Leyden. The following year, a French abbot, Nollet, employed a charged Leyden jar and "shocked" a group of monks who were holding hands in a circle. Suddenly, electricity was becoming quite fashionable.

Within a few years, electricity was used to heal sicknesses and later to generate a spark to ignite barrels of gunpowder.

Then, in 1786, when Luigi Galvani discovered that electricity flowed within animals, it was confirmed that a "divine life force" existed within us. This revelation surprised the scientific community and in part placated the Church.

By 1800, Alessandro Volta had created his "voltaic pile," which was, in essence, a storage battery composed of alternate layers of copper and zinc. When immersed in water supplemented with a little acid, the voltaic pile produced a continuous flow of electricity.

Then, in 1820, H. C. Oersted, of Copenhagen, discovered that electric current through a wire affected a nearby compass needle. His discovery, in turn, led Frenchman André Ampère to realize the magnetic field. By 1825, William Sturgeon, of England, wound a live wire around a bar of soft iron, creating the first electromagnet.

In 1831, Michael Faraday rotated a metal disk between the poles of a horseshoe magnet and produced electricity. Then, in 1849, Professor Floris Nollet, of Brussels, devised the process of electrically separating hydrogen and oxygen from water—the process called electrolysis.

Later, in 1857, an Englishman, Frederick Holmes, created a large-scale magneto-electric generator system, which caused carbon rods to glow incandescently, creating the arc lamp.

By 1871, Zénobie Gramme, a French engineer, employed all this previous research, plus the work of a Dane, Sören Hjorth, to produce electricity "dynamically," yielding the dynamo-electric generator.

Once, when I was about fifteen years old, while staying in the Jura Mountains, I witnessed a most violent Thunder Storm, the loudness of which was most frightful, as if its rumblings echoed from various quarters of the Heavens. I remained throughout the storm, watching its progress with both curiosity and delight. When a great jagged Light occurred, I saw a stream of fire issue from a beautiful old oak, which with the flash of light disappeared, leaving nothing but a charred stump.

Before this storm I was not unacquainted with the more obvious Laws of Nature. I had been well instructed in the subject of Electricity and Galvanism, which when first introduced, was at once new and astonishing to me.

Thus, I betook myself to Mathematics and the branches of Study appertaining to that science, those built upon secure foundations worthy of my consideration. But now, a Modern System of Science had been introduced which possessed much greater Powers than the ancient and antik methods. Science required an absolute knowledge of a topic - a Subjective Knowledge, drawn from first-hand experience.

Science and God

Even in the enlightened times of the early nineteenth century, scientific works were still evaluated with suspicion. The courts mandated that all unexplainable physical phenomena could only be recognized as proof of the manifestation of God's work on Earth. Any deviation from this Christian thought or any consideration of nature's independent workings (later known as evolution) was labeled as heresy and was followed by the appropriate punishment.

The Scientist need dissect his Objective, he must anatomise and name all its parts and be able to understand completely the function of its most minute process.

Though I followed the standard routines of early 19th Century Universities in Switzerland and Germany, my favorite studies were self-taught.

Saturday, 27 August 1808. — Age 17.
— INGOLSTADT. UNIVERSITY.

At the age of seventeen I enrolled as a Student at the University of Ingolstadt. Here, I could study the works of my favorite Alchemists. I excitedly anticipated my forth-coming class in Science and Medicine.

Sunday, 4 September 1808. — GENEVA.

After only a few days in Ingolstadt, I was summoned back to my home in Geneva, where I found my beloved Elizabeth had contracted the Scarlet Fever; the degree of her illness was severe. She had been watchfully attended by my own dear Mother, who three days later fell to the pestilent disease. Upon my Mother's death-bed,

Equipment and Materials

Despite social, political, and religious obstacles, the nineteenth century scientist was also expected to overcome any practical problems. Before he could conduct any experimental research, he had to acquire the proper equipment and apparatus. The only way to do this was to design it.

Not only was he responsible for inventing equipment, he also had to supervise the fabrication of every piece. Next, the scientist would gather base chemicals, mineral ores, natural elements, herbs, and medicines, which he processed into raw chemicals and compounds.

The scientist needed a place to conduct his work, a laboratory, and a source of energy to drive his newly built apparatus. Energy in 1816 was supplied by human, animal, wind, or water power. The earliest steam engines had just been invented and were terribly dangerous, often exploding unexpectedly. Although the energy properties of electricity had been recognized for centuries, it was in the nineteenth century that electricity was finally harnessed to operate small equipment. It was this invisible source of energy that offered the greatest promise for the future.

She joined Elizabeth's hand to my own and bade we swear our troth. Mother resigned herself to death with hopes of meeting us at some later time in another, more peaceful world.

Thursday, 22 September 1808. — GENEVA.

The time arrived when I left to continue my studies at Ingolstadt. The day of my departure was spent happily with Elizabeth and Clerval, my two dearest friends.

Soon we three were joined by my grieving Father. After much persuasion, we all said "farewell," and I climbed into the Carriage which was to convey me away. I kept the image of my sweet Elizabeth's enchanting face which lent some small degree of consolation.

Friday, 30 September 1808. — INGOLSTADT UNIVERSITY.

Shortly after my arrival I delivered Letters of Introduction to the University and called on several of my principle Professors. Upon entering my apartments, I was greeted by an amiable young student, Franz Kulig, who despite his short stature and slightly bent frame, proved to be quite knowledgeable. Perhaps

Surgical Implements.

it was chance which led my reluctant steps to the chambers of
M. Krempe, Professor of Natural
History. He was an uncouth man,
but deeply embued in the secrets of
his Science.

Professor Krempe questioned my previous independent studies. I mentioned the names of the Alchemist
authors whom I had studied.
He suggested that I had utterly
wasted my time on the work of these
men, and that I had burdened my
memory with irrelevant theories and
useless names. "These fancies," he
replied, "which you have so greedily
imbibed, are a thousand years old, and
as musty as they are ancient." So saying,
he stepped aside and compiled a list
of Books treating Natural Philosophy,
which he insisted I procure.

After mentioning my required attend-
ance at the Chemistry lectures, to
commence the following week, of a fellow
professor, M. Waldman, he then dismissed me with a wave of his hand.
With a muddled head, I returned
to my quarters.

Could I change the discoveries of
recent Scientific Enquirers for the
dreams of forgotten Alchemists?
The old Masters of Science sought
immortality and power; such views,
although futile, were grand.

Commentary on Franz and
the Women in Victor's Life

Because of sketchy details in letters and vague insinuations from Victor's notes, the character of Franz Kulig remains an enigma. We do know that Franz was a fellow at Ingolstadt University Medical College.

Victor also suggests that Franz was of short stature and possibly had a physical handicap. The young Kulig may have been inflicted with shortness and twisted legs, perhaps as a result of rickets, polio, or some other disease of the time. The image of Frankenstein's assistant as a hunchback is a theatrical one, but a deformity of this degree was never mentioned.

Victor Frankenstein lived with his parents in an upper-class and aristocratic family, the eldest of three brothers. His cousin-fiancée, Elizabeth, lived nearby; her family, once estranged became closer, and they visited frequently. Both families maintained servants, the most prominent being Justine Moritz, a young local woman.

Victor was always a serious young man whose grim literary endeavors revealed his dark side. As a boy he was fond of poetry, nature, and science and adroit with toys, automata, gadgets, and inventions. Victor was privately tutored at home in the Oxford classics of Latin, Greek, and maths. Later, at university, he specialized in science and medicine, with plans to pursue those professions.

The circumstances of Victor's sexual experiences are openly speculative. He grew up in a male-dominated household, and besides a few female servants, Victor's strongest feminine influence was from his ailing mother. When he was seven, he first met his cousin Elizabeth, who was five or six years old at the time. They became betrothed a few years later, when she was fifteen and Victor was sixteen years old.

The opposite sex did not seem to be of much interest to Victor when he was young, although the lonely days at university may have changed his opinion.

Monday, 3 October 1808. —

I attended Professor Waldman's lectures in part to pass the idle time and partly from curiosity. Once he entered the Lecture Hall, I could see that this professor was unlike his colleague. He appeared to be about fifty years of age with an air of the greatest benevolence. M. Waldman's lectures on Chemistry were curiously original.

He began by recapitulating the history of the science, then went on to discuss the various discoveries made in most recent times, including the works of Sir Humphrey Davey, Laplace and the late Lord Cavendish. After a short demonstration of a few preparatory experiments, he concluded with a discussion on modern Chemistry, the details of which I shall never forget. "The ancient teachers of chemistry promised impossibilities and performed nothing. The modern masters promise very little; they know metals cannot be transmuted and that the Elixir of Life is a Chimera."

He continued: "The Philosophers whose hands seem only made to dabble in dirt — and whose eyes to pore over the Microscope or Crucible, have indeed performed miracles. They reveal Nature and show her hiding places. They have discovered how blood courses through the human body, have analyzed the air we breathe through

During this period of eleven months (October 1808 to September 1809), Victor Frankenstein's journal lapses considerably, with few entries. Omissions are probably due to increased scholastic studies. Victor continued his studies in physics, anatomy, biology, surgery, chemistry, and medicine.

The use of male cadavers in anatomy studies was very common. These corpses were provided by the police. They were often the lifeless bodies of recently executed criminals or murdered transients. Female cadavers were less common: there were fewer women transients, and those who were victims of murder were usually known. The morals of the day dictated that an unclothed female body, even a dead one, should not be viewed by young men.

their Studies, mocking the invisible world with its own shadows."

Treading in the steps already marked, I will pioneer a new way, explore unknown powers, and unfold to the world the deepest mysteries of Creation.

Tuesday, 4 October 1808. - MY APARTMENT.

When I returned to my quarters, young Franz had taken it upon him- self to thoughtfully prepare a cold dinner and to procure an admirable vintage Rhine. Unable to close my eyes all night, my mind was in turmoil as the dark succumbed to dawn — I finally slept.

Wednesday, 5 October 1808.

I awoke from my yesternight's sleep as from a Dream, resolute to return to my Ancient Studies and to devote myself to the Science for which I possessed a natural talent. The Natural Scientist should apply every branch of that Philosophy to his Magnus Opus, including the Sciences of Physics and Mathematics.

This evening I visited the home of Professor M. Waldman; he introduced me to his only daughter, Christine, aged 12, quite a beautiful young lady.

During this era, many still considered the heart as to be the seat of the human soul, that which governed man's emotions, passions, and thoughts.

Eighteenth century doctor George E. Stahl of Halle University rejected both the chemical and mechanical schools. He asserted instead that "the Living Processes were directed by Man's sensitive Soul," a philosophy which was a precurser to psychology and the theory of unconscious, psychosomatic causes of illness.

She brought us some coffee and
sherry. The Professor's manners in
private were even more mild and attractive than in public, and he listened
with attention to my narrative concerning
past scientific experiences and studies.
M. Waldman then took me into his
private Laboratory and explained the
uses of his various Machines, in-
structing me as to what I ought to
procure, promising me the use of his
own once I advanced far enough not
to ruin their mechanisms. He gave
me a list of books which I had
requested. I then took my leave.

The weather suddenly turned un-
seasonably cold. Although it is
only early Autumn, the smell of
snow is in the air. Upon arriving
at my rooms, a pleasant letter was
delivered from my beloved Elizabeth.
Admittedly, during these days of
research and study, my thoughts
have wandered far from home and friends.

We talked of the experiments of
Sir Humphrey Davey, and his
use of Electrical Energy to animate
muscles; and of Dr. Erasmus
Darwin who preserved a piece of
vermicelli in a glass case, until, by
some means it began to move. Thus,
after all, life could be given.
Perhaps too a Corpse could be re-
animated. Galvanism had hinted
at such a thing, which led me to think
that possibly the component parts
of a creature might be manufactured, brought together, and embued
with life's vital warmth.

34.

Sunday, 19 September 1809. – Yr. 2 at University.

Almost a year has passed since my last Journal entry, during which time I paid no visits to Geneva, but was engaged, heart and soul, in the pursuit of many Physical, Chemical and Anatomical discoveries. The summer months were most beautiful, the vines yielded a luxuriant fruit. I was the recipient of endless letters from my beloved Elizabeth; they reflected her anxiety on my behalf.

I continue to attend University lectures on Physics and Medicine, but the Anatomy and Physiology demonstrations capture my most rapt attention.

During all other waking hours I focus my attention solely on improving my Chemical Apparatus, building the Instruments of Physical Mechanism, or discovering some Chemical Formula. The advances I have made awarded me some admiration among the other students and faculty here at the university.

With school completed, and his doctor's certificate earned, Victor had also received part of his family inheritance. He used this money to finance his scientific works. Victor left the university and moved into a larger, more suitable apartment in town. He prepared for his "great work" by leasing a single room on the upper most floor of an old building.

While Victor performed certain anatomical experiments on available cadavers, he also designed specific tools and equipment with which he hoped to eventually conduct his newly found "secret-of-life process."

Franz Kulig, Victor's friend and a fellow student, was an intelligent university researcher. He acted as Victor's scientific assistant and also attended to many of his daily and personal needs.

The cold weather during this period cloaked Victor in a deep malaise, a sickness of both mind and body. A few entries in his journal suggest that he may have contracted influenza or bronchitis.

Monday, 20 September 1809.

One phenomenon which has particularly attracted my interest is the
Anatomical Structure of the
Human frame, or indeed, any animal.
I have realized that to examine
the source of Life, I must first
consider its antithesis — Death —
and in so doing need observe the
natural decay of the human body.
Through my courses of study and
the careful dissection of various
Cadavers provided (somewhat dis-
reputably due to local laws), I have
learned the basic Physical Mech-
anics of Anatomy, the components
of humanity.

38.

Saturday, 25 September 1809. —

I have never been impressed by the supposed horrors of the Super-natural. Darkness has no effect upon my fancy, and to me, a church-yard is merely the receptacle of bodies deprived of life — food for the worm. My studies force me to spend days and nights in Cemetery Vaults and Charnel-Houses. Here, I have witnessed how the fine form of Man turns to waste. I have beheld Death as it succeeds

the blooming cheek of Life, and I have seen how the Worm inherits the wonders of the eye and brain.

Suddenly, a wondrous Light broke in upon me, a Light so glorious, a revelation so brilliant, that I became dizzy with the potential it held. It is surprising that so many Men of Genius have overlooked this scientific process — and that I alone, a mere neophyte, should discover so astonishing a Secret. These writings may appear to be the Visions of a Mad-man.

Not so, after days and nights of incredible labour. I am fatigued, but I have discovered the cause of generation and of life. Nay! Moreover I am capable of Animating Lifeless Matter. This discovery is so over-whelming that I have for some time hesitated to employ it ...

40.

I keep my Workshop of Creations. In order to attend to the details of my Experiments, I am forced to employ the Dissecting Room and the Slaughter House to furnish the appropriate Lifeless Frames. Often, I turned with loathing from my vile occupation, while still urged on by my eagerness to conclude.

My Colleague Franz has entered into my employ.

But I do possess the power to bestow Animated Life, and therefore must prepare a "Frame," a lifeless body, to receive this gift.

_____

6 January, 1813. — Anatomical Studies.

The Cold Rains have turned to Snow, and it seems ironic that this joyous holiday season is to be coupled with the most foul practice of my Carnal work. This Evening I collected Bones from the Charnal Houses; then I explored the tremendous Secrets of the Human Frame. In a Solitary Chamber, or more aptly a Cell, which I leased at the top of a House,

Medicines were relatively uncommon in these times, but folk remedies made of natural herbal teas and poultices and mineral compounds, which were applied to the skin, were generally available. In most towns, an apothecary or herbalist sold the cures, while in rural areas, these potions were provided by an elderly local woman who possessed a knowledge of healing. The prescriptions were often accompanied by a ritual prayer or incantation. In fact, the only preventive medicine available was prayer. Sickness was still believed to be the infestation of the human body by demons.

13 February 1813 — Weather Changes.
Today the weather appears particularly bleak; the sky is overcast.

The coming of snow seems inevitable, and despite my cough and high fever, I shall persist with my occupation. It is, during these dark months, my only pursuit. This singular passion causes me to neglect those friends who are absent, so many miles away, those

I have not seen for so long a time. I know my silence disquiets them. But, I cannot tear my thoughts away from this loath- some task. This work has hold of my imagination, swallow- ing all of her preoccupations. My Father's many letters are not the least reproachful of my negligence in Correspondence, though he has enquired about my occupations more particularly than before.

My physical health now suffers seriously. I know not whether this malaise, which has wrested me to my Couch, is a result of my extended working hours, or, as my associate Franz insists, a poor diet and lack of adequate rest.

Friday, 2 April 1813. — SPRINGTIME.

Several months have again elapsed since my last Journal entry. During that period I lay help- less with a severe attack of the Influenza and other painful and spirit-evoking maladies. During my fevered Hallucinations I saw the face of my dear Elizabeth, my friend Clerval, my Father and most frequently the face of my lovely departed Mother.

II

The Laboratory

Frankenstein's Discovery of
His Family's Ancestral Castle
and His Preparations for
the Great Work

46.

Thursday, 4 August 1814. — A year Elapses from last entry.

There have been fewer travellers on the Continent these last years since Britain joined the coalition against Napoleon. With the Emperor's exile, our countryside has become terrorized by roving Bandits, Soldiers and Thieves. There is a scarcity of food and bread because the roads and bridges have been blown up! King Louis XVIII of France has returned to the throne. He and his Bourbon supporters continue battle against the Bonaparte supporters.

Wednesday, 24 August 1814. — Travel Plans.

My health has returned. With Franz's help, I plan to travel from Ingolstadt to venture North to my ancestral lands at Goldstadt, near Darmstadt. I have visited there only once during my Childhood; at that time the estates were in an awful state of disrepair.

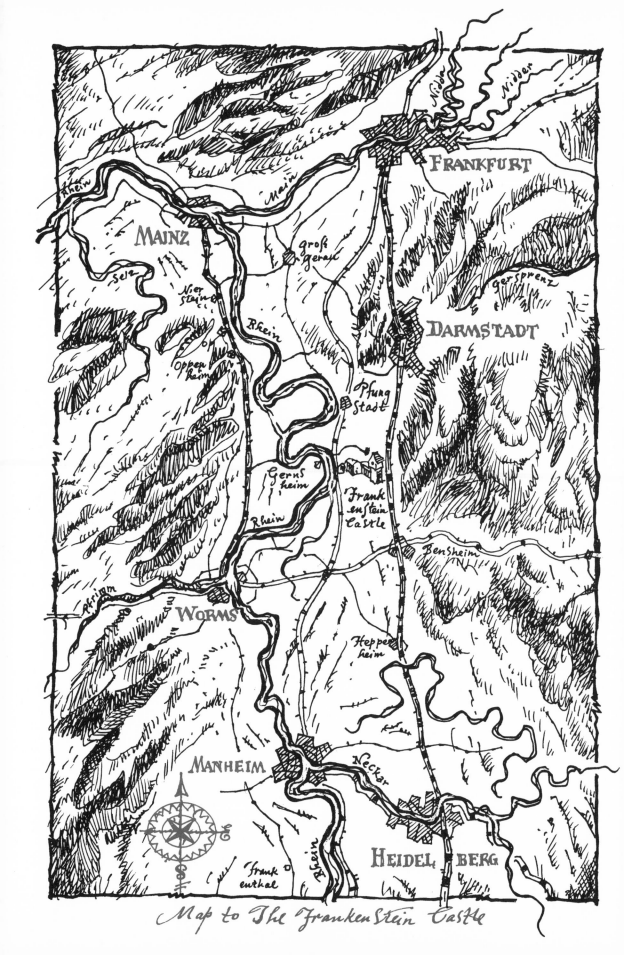

Map to The Frankenstein Castle

Friday, 26 August 1814. — Upon the River.

Our journey carried us Northward from Ingolstadt, along the Naäb River to its juncture with the Danube. From here we continued along the river, through the beautiful Bavarian countryside toward Nürnberg and Bamberg. Despite the presence of some odious travelling companions, our voyage was rather un-remarkable. Even in these bucolic surroundings talk of the War and the destruction left in its path has reached our ears. Franz remarked that his elder brother had been conscripted by the Polish Army.

Tuesday, 30 August 1814. — Upon the River.

Today we continued our journey on the Main River and stopped at Würzburg for Customs inspection. We then went to Aschaffenberg. Here, rather than continuing onward by boat to Frankfort, we disembarked. I purchased a Diligence and horses, then travelled cross-country through the mountain passes to the city of Darmstadt.

The Castle Frankenstein

The Castle Frankenstein has been part of the Darmstadt district for over a thousand years—as the family's feudal fortress, a refugee hospital, a place of sanctuary, and an alchemical laboratory for the Counts of Hesse.

During the 1720s and 1730s, the castle became the property of a German soldier named Euler who defected to the French Army. While he was away at the wars, his deranged wife sold off the castle's treasures, including expensive gold and silver religious relics, furniture, paintings, parquet flooring, stones and bricks from the walls, and copper shingles from the roof—all to maintain her "court of lovers." The furnishings and items that she was unable to sell were eventually burned as firewood.

The castle soon fell to disrepair. Mrs. Euler died in 1740, after her husband.

The next period of the Castle's occupation came with Victor and Franz, from 1813 to 1817.

During the late eighteenth century, interest in the Castle Frankenstein was again revived with the arrival of a small group of literary pilgrims, lovers of Gothic ruins and nature. The group, known as the Darmstadt Circle was guided by its patroness: the Countess of Hesse, wife of King Ludwig IX. The members of the group were generally amateur writers who had been influenced by the newly popular English Gothic literary movement. This little gathering of bookish intelligentsia also attracted a few celebrities, such as the beautiful Princess Louisa of Mecklenburg-Strelitz, future Queen of Prussia, and the German writer Goethe, who read his verses and discussed his work-in-progress, *Faust*.

As the Castle Frankenstein became a popular tourist attraction, King Ludwig III ordered extensive restorations to be made starting in the early 1890s and continuing through 1912-13.

Friday, 2 September 1814. — City of Darmstadt.

The city of Darmstadt has grown
into a bustling and popular city.
From Darmstadt we drove the mares
through the mountains and into the Rhine
Valley near Eberstadt-Pfungstadt
and the village of Goldstadt.
We arrived at the ancestral lands
at sunset.
The mountains and clouds were illuminated by the Sun's fiery glow. The last
hues of day reflected in the water.
The Hills were covered with lush
forests and crowned by lonely crumbling
Castles. With the setting Sun
came the Winds, which curtailed our
travels.

Sweeping upward from there, through
rugged hills, was the silhouette of
a double-towered Castle which
lay in ruins teetering on a tremendous
precipice. And beyond that, high
above the river, on the summit of Great
Magnet Mountain — stood the familial
Castle Frankenstein!

Though now in near ruin, to me it
appeared to be most beautiful.

Castle Frankenstein. Bridge Tower

<u>Saturday Morning, 3 September 1814.</u>

Quitting the village of Nieder-Beerbach at the mountain's base, after much effort, we maneuvered our Horses and Diligence up the long abandoned Tyrolian Road toward the Castle. The hour was late as we finally arrived at the overgrown courtyard of my family's ancestral manse. Despite the coldness of night, excitement prevailed as we approached the crumbling, shadowy battlements and moss-covered bridgework of the castle's entrance.

We made our way across the Court-yard toward one of the last two standing Massive Stone Towers.

Franz and I entered Castle Frankenstein through the main portal. With Lanterns held high, we stepped over the great unhinged Door which had been tossed aside some years before by local Peasant Treasure Hunters.

We scrambled over accumulated years of growth and clutter into a high-vaulted Central Room, which years before had served as the Main Gathering place.

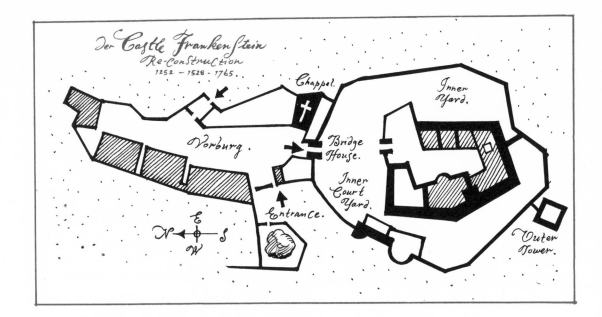

The First Doctor Frankenstein
(Seventeenth Century)

Perhaps the most famous of the early Frankensteins was actually an *adopted* member of the family. In 1673, as Louis XIV's Catholic Army of France ravaged the German Empire, a Lutheran minister named Dipple and his pregnant wife took sanctuary at the Castle Frankenstein, which had then become a war hospital.

Johann Konrad Dipple was born at the castle, and as was acceptable for the times, appended the name von Frankenstein to his own name. Aside from his five sisters and two brothers, the youth Konrad was said to have been a very scholarly lad whose interests ranged from theology, natural philosophy, medicine, and chemistry to the elusive art of alchemy. The local citizens believed that his material success was due to his having sold his soul to the Devil.

It is said that Konrad upset the students and faculty at the Universities of Giessen and later Strasbourg (1694) by expounding on scientific theology, astrology, and other spiritualistic pursuits. He was considered by many to possess the powers of healing and visionary prophecy. It is said that he was forced to flee unexpectedly from Strasbourg one night after some "serious incident," which gossip

Sunday, 4 September 1814. — The Castle.

In the cold light of morning, the Castle's design recalled centuries past. Outside the walls are the defensive Ramparts and Round Towers, once used for housing Gunpowder. Inside the gate are Porticoes and Observation Posts, all surrounded by a Moat and Drawbridge. Within the walls, the Castle separates into two distinct Sections.

I recall my Father telling me that several centuries earlier the Family had feuded over inheritances, then split the castle into two separate parts.

Both families lived in this divided Castle for over 250 years. To the northeast is the older Kern Tower, with self-contained Living Quarters, Kitchen, Stable and Wine Cellar.

In another Courtyard are a group of fortress-like Quarters built into the Wall, wherein the family Chapel may be found. Built upon a much earlier Foundation, the Chapel contains the Graves and Effigies of many of my early Ancestors.

I chose the abandoned Chapel for our Laboratory. Its high Ceiling and intact Lead Roof make it the most satisfactory work area. Also adjacent are several Rooms — ideal Sleeping Quarters for Franz and myself.

1252 – 1328 AD.
The Original Frankenstein Castle.

suggests was a body-snatching affair. After this scandalous escape from Strasbourg, Konrad Dipple von Frankenstein returned to his home near Darmstadt to concentrate on his alchemical studies.

At this same time, the Landgrave, Count Ernst Ludwig of Hesse (1667-1739), a minor Prince of Darmstadt, had the dream of transforming his petty principality into the splendors of Louis XIV's golden Versailles. By this time, the Landgrave Prince had nearly bankrupted his Darmstadt treasury, so he hired the services of several local alchemists in an attempt to replenish his gold losses.

The entire Rhine district, around Frankenstein's domain, became an alchemical community. Practitioners of the art worked day and night for the Landgrave, and their laboratories were everywhere. The raw materials of sulfur, mercury, antimony, copper, and others were employed to discover the secret formula for making the "Philosopher's Stone."

Because of the alchemists' sloppy processes and their use of the most impure ingredients, these gold experiments proved quite unsuccessful. Huge amounts of the Landgrave Prince's money were squandered on this chimeric goal, and little was accomplished to restock his money vaults.

Upon Dipple's return to the Darmstadt district, he was introduced to some revolutionary (though more ancient) alchemical processes. He became fired with renewed enthusiasm, and with dreams of possibly purchasing the now abandoned Castle Frankenstein for his laboratory experiments, Konrad resettled in the vicinity.

After months of intensive alchemical work, Konrad declared in 1701 that he had achieved success. By dissolving "the Philosopher's Stone" into 50 parts of molten silver and mercury, Dipple claimed, he had produced the very purest of gold, which quite delighted the Landgrave Prince.

But as with all wondrous events, certain traditions are expected to be observed. Alchemical lore and legends declare that for the philosopher to prevent a curse, he must never use his knowledge, wisdom, or gold for any personal gain.

Konrad ignored the legend, and with the Landgrave's payment he purchased a large land estate. Almost immediately his luck changed—

Our House-Maid, the castle's only other occupant, resides in the Kitchen, located across the Courtyard.

More so than the romantic remnants of a bygone age, I was impressed by the marvelous view. This first morning when I looked out from the Castle's Tower, it was like an

_____

Opera Curtain had been raised, and there before me, shrouded by a milky haze, lay the vast Plains of the Rhine. The River glittered like molten silver. From my Aerie, the Steeples of so many Villages punctuated the Landscape, while Donnersberg's Thunder Mountain provided a backdrop off in the distance.

Views on a clear day may reach up to 40 miles.

_____

Sunday, 4 September 1814. — Frankenstein Castle.

Franz and I immediately set forth repairing our ruinous and disheveled new Household. After a few days of occupancy, several local Village Authorities... the Burger Meister, Herr Kneisel, Constable Blum and Reverend de Pouque - paid us a visit. Although our provisions were meagre, we accommodated them with a pleasant cup of tea.

for the worse. It is said that while celebrating he accidentally knocked over the jar containing "the Philosopher's Stone," which was destroyed, while the secret formula, which had taken years to perfect, was lost.

After three years of fruitless experiments, Konrad was unable to reproduce the secret of his alchemical results. Defeated, he moved away from the Darmstadt district and wandered about Europe for the next twenty-five years (1704-29).

Konrad Dipple von Frankenstein eventually settled in Berlin, the new capital of the Kingdom of Prussia under Frederick I. He soon came under the sponsorship of the King to act as his Royal Scientist and promote research in various subjects. Dipple now concentrated on his "universal elixer," a medicine to cure (nearly) all of man's ills.

Dipple's most famous Berlin discovery came when he heated to very high temperatures bones, dried blood, scrap hair, and other ingredients, mixing them with scrap iron and potash; he produced a beautiful blue chemical called potassium ferro-cyanide. This substance quickly became the base pigment for the artist's color Prussian blue, or Berlin blue (1724).

An additional experiment, adding sulfuric acid to potassium ferro-cyanide, produced hydrocyanic, or Prussic acid, one of the most potent poisons known, which even in tiny quantities causes death by paralysis of the heart and spinal cord.

Mistaken for a spy in Berlin in 1707, Konrad Dipple was imprisoned, but he was eventually released. He quickly emigrated to Holland, and there, for seven years, he continued his scientific experiments at the University of Leyden. His hurried exits and escapes from these various countries all seem very suspicious, and no explanation for the reason of his activities is available.

Once again he fled from Holland to Denmark, where he was well received at Altona and had the title "Royal Councilor" bestowed upon him. But after having written and published several derogatory pamphlets on the local politicians, he incurred the wrath of Count Reventlow, and once again Dipple found himself imprisoned—this time for *life*.

Now Konrad's scientific writings were publicly burned, and he was securely tied and thrown into the dark, wet dungeon of the Castle Hammarshus. Fortunately, he was released after ten or so years, as his

The Guests were satisfied with our intentions and welcomed us to the district. They asked if I was familiar with the Castle's curious thousand year history, and after I related my account of the story, the Gentlemen from Town supplemented it with the exploits of Conrad Dipple von Franken-stein, and other of my more illustrious Forebearers.

Subsequently, they gave us names of several Workmen from the Village, for building and repairs.

Shortly thereafter, our tiny staff arrived and, overseen by Franz, set about their duties, leaving me the time to focus solely on My Experiment.

As Franz looked after the House-hold duties and acquisitions, I began the long and complicated task of outlining the procedures necessary to conduct my Works.

My first consideration was "The Process!" I require some highly detailed and technically specialized Scientific Equipment with with to perform these Processes.

Therefore, I will devote the next several months to the careful design of specific equipment, much of which is new to the world of man.

extraordinary medical reputation had come to the attention of the Queen of Denmark. He soon became her personal physician and achieved the standing of a miracle healer. As Dipple's fame became international, it spread even to the court of Russia's Catherine the Great (1725-27), who wished to summon him to St. Petersberg.

He finally accepted service to King Frederick I of Sweden, who suffered from some strange, incurable malady. Konrad's diagnosis was that "disease does not originate in a malfunctioning of the body; but rather, the spirit must be healed first, by psychic or suggestive means, and only then will the body be restored with the aid of chemistry." Apparently, this process worked.

All during his stay in Sweden, Dipple remained controversial. He was called the Messiah of the Nobility, while also being suspected of being a Russian spy. Later, after he was refused the bishopric of Uppsala, in 1729 he returned to his home in Germany. It had been over twenty-five years since Konrad had seen his homeland.

For all his life Dipple remained a bachelor and stayed faithful to his family and relatives. Eventually, he moved into his brother's large mansion, a few miles from Castle Frankenstein, where he continued conducting alchemical experiments. Soon, his work became manifest and Dipple rediscovered his secret alchemical process, which he then offered to his old patron, the Landgrave of Hesse, in return for the Castle Frankenstein and all its domains—for himself and his heirs.

Negotiations for the castle, with the Landgrave of Hesse, eventually broke down, and nothing ever came of them. Dipple continued his alchemical works, and in 1733 he published a work that declared his discovery of a longevity formula and that it would prolong his own life to age 135!

By 1734, less than one year after his prophecy, Dipple von Frankenstein was found dead in the rooms of a friend's palace. The corpse was cold and rigid, he'd been foaming at the mouth, and part of his face had turned blue!

The authorities declaired Dipple's death unnatural, and though it was locally believed he was killed by the Devil, it is most likely that he had been poisoned, or else he committed suicide by poison. His body was buried at the Chapel of Laasphe, in Wittgenstein, from where it has since mysteriously vanished.

Wednesday, 26 October 1814. — The Work
Begins.

During these next weeks I will devote all my knowledge, education and experience to my Work. The Purpose of my Scientific Adventure is now within my grasp. I can almost sense the presence of the Ghost of old Conrad Dipple, guiding my hand in its Design. Franz also continues to prove his Scientific ingenuity, and daily displays his capabilities in various useful ways. But Franz has a darker Nature which surfaces on occasion, especially during periods of his Melancholy.

Saturday, 29 October 1814. — Preparing
the Work.

It is a warm and pleasant Autumn day and my spirits are boosted, anticipating the forthcoming Work. Franz has driven the Diligence into Darmstadt, where he will remain for several days to make arrangements with a number of Craftsmen which I've hired for their Services and Materials.

III

Equipment & Materials

Acquisition and Construction of
Laboratory Apparatus

Gear Haus
in ruins.

MILL HOUSE.

Gears

WHEEL

Mill Wheel.
Repaired

Gear Haus.
Restored.

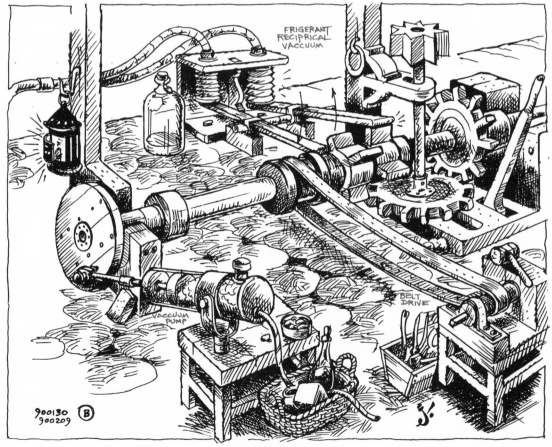

FRIGERANT
RECIPRICAL
VACCUUM

VACCUUM
PUMP

BELT
DRIVE

900130 Ⓑ
900209

Monday, 16 January 1815. — Preparing the Work.

Over the past weeks, I met with a number of Local Craftsmen in the Village and elsewhere to enquire about fabricating various Pieces of Apparatus, Furniture and Tools which we need.

Not long after disclosing the Designs of my Apparatus to the Craftsmen, the Local Townspeople began to discuss the purpose for which they believed these items would be employed. Considering the past infamy heaped upon the Frankenstein name and Castle over the centuries, they concluded that my work was that of the Devil.

Friday, 20 January 1815. — Designs for Equipment.

My Mechanical Devices were inspired by the contrivances of Agostino Ramelli (1588) and Vitruvius. They will operate as "Driving Mechanisms" for my Laboratory Equipment. The Windlass, the Water-Wheel and the Electricity Generator, plus variances on Pumps, Vacuums and Reciprocals, promise to provide all of the Force needed. In recent days we have repaired the Castle's demolished Water Chute and Wheel.

The Industrial Revolution

The period from the late eighteenth to the early nineteenth century was a time in world history marked by a rapid cultural transition from an agricultural to an industrial society. European expansionism, scientific and technical inventiveness, economic sophistication, and the availability of more natural resources all combined during these years to provide new business opportunities.

During the later decades of the 1700s, inventive capitalists developed the factory system, which mass-produced cheap textiles and other products for supply world markets. The smelting of iron in 1709 and the development of the steam engine in 1781 led to wider expansion of the railroads and canal transportation, which in turn could increasean industry's marketplace considerably.

By the 1830s, most of Europe was linked by transport to new raw supplies and markets. Improvements in food supplies, sanitation, and medicine created population growths, and by the 1850s a large new labor force and greater consumer demand had developed.

In the early 1800s, during Victor Frankenstein's time, the Industrial Revolution was still in its formative stages. Despite the new technology and therefore new machines, most manufactured items were still largely made by hand. The craftsmen and technicians of Darmstadt whom Dr. Frankenstein commissioned were considered highly advanced for their day.

I am reminded that in earliest times, Mills were the first service industries, and flour was a relatively rare commodity. Also curious is that our Saxon word for an aristocrat, "Lord," means "Loaf giver." But we shall not employ ours for grinding grain; rather to drive Wheels, Cogs, Cranks and Cams to run the Mill.

Tuesday, 21 February 1815. — Preparation of the Laboratory.

The most immediate necessities, at this time, are our basic Human comforts and requirements. Repairs to the Roof, securing Doors and Windows against cold Weather, and the provision of Wood and Coal for heat and cooking are of the utmost importance. We constantly venture into the village for Materials and Supplies. Those items which cannot be obtained in the Village require a visit to Darmstadt, which can consume several hours and often several days of my precious time!

Despite my hectic schedule, I continue to spend every possible hour working to design the procedures and Equipment for my great Experiment.

Equipment

Rigid metal tubing was often fabricated from copper, tin, or silver. Most came in thick diameters, and it generally contained a seam along its length. This type of tubing was regularly used for making musical instruments, tubular canisters, and casings or rigid distillation tubing for stills.

Wide flexible hosing for use as water hoses or fire hoses was made by sewing strips of canvas into long sleeves, then waterproofing them with tar. (Rubber waterproofing wasn't discovered until Mackintosh invented his water-resistant fabric in the 1820s.)

Narrow, flexible tubing was made by knitting a tube, then dipping it into bee's wax, India rubber, varnish, chicle-gum base (in a vinegar wash), or egg white.

The first sculptural anatomical specimens appeared in the seventeenth century by an artist, Dr. Ruysch, of Holland. He preserved human skeletons, bladder stones, veins, arteries, and organs by injecting colored wax and other substances into them. Czar Peter the Great of Russia was so emotionally moved by Ruych's collection, particularly a preserved child, that he promptly bought the whole exhibit for 30,000 Dutch florins.

During the seventeenth century there were iatro-chemists, who believed that the body was a vessel, a "test tube," in which chemicals did the work, and there were iatro-mechanists, who saw the human body as a machine.

The chemical school believed that fermentation of food in the body caused all the vital actions. The mechanical school, primarily Italian, studied the workings of the skeleton and muscles, noting that the lungs functioned as bellows and the teeth as scissors, for example—all working to result in the body's movement.

My associate, Franz, has proved
himself very astute in the design
and fabrication of our Laboratory
Apparatus. Thus far he has
most easily accomplished, and even
improved upon, many of the
applications which I have merely
conceived of in sketches.

Ash.
<u>Wednesday</u> —, <u>March 1815</u> – Springtime.

Our Haus-fräulein, Magda, amused
us with an old local Legend.
At her home, this day, her grandmother warned that she must depart
from our Castle Walls before dark,
and if not, then at least before the Village
Church Bells strike midnight.
Otherwise, her grandmother cautioned,
she would be punished and tormented
by the many Dæmons who waited
in the Woods this Ash Wednesday
night.

These weeks of early Spring are
marked by brilliant sunshine.
Our household has attracted several
Locals in need of Medical service,
to which I employ the "magical remedy"
of the French Physician, François
Rabelais: namely – the Essence of
Laughter.

Rabelais confessed that he administered his <u>"Medicine of Humor"</u>
successfully to his Patients, upon
whom it exerted a decidedly
therapeutic effect.

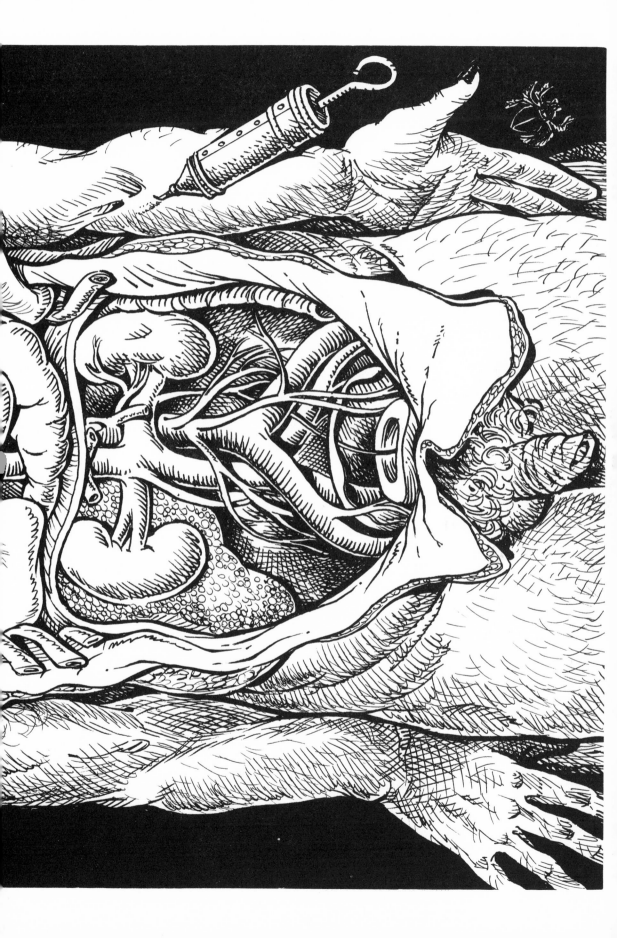

Blood Transfusions

The process of bleeding a patient to relieve the bad humors from his system was popular from earliest times up to and including the 1880s.

The first blood transfusions began in Paris in 1667. Initially, the blood was drawn from calves, dogs, sheep, oxen, and occasionally men. Hollow hypodermic needles did not exist in these earliest days, but feather quills, hollow birds' bones, and silver tubes were employed. There were no flexible rubber or plastic tubes for connections, so the windpipes of ducks and the arteries and ureters of lambs, oxen, and calves were used. Syringes and plastic bags also didn't exist, so these clever technologists made use of urinary bladders and pouches made from animal skins.

Early medical texts describe how blood transfusions were performed by drawing off pouchfuls of dog's blood, then replacing the human blood with this fresh fluid into an opened vein. Many patients died, but occasionally some survived. In these cases it's doubtful that any of the blood actually entered the veins.

Around 1817, when it was realized that transfusions more often than not caused death, the process was banned by the French Parliament, England's Royal Society, and the Pope. As a result, no transfusions were recorded for the next 150 years.

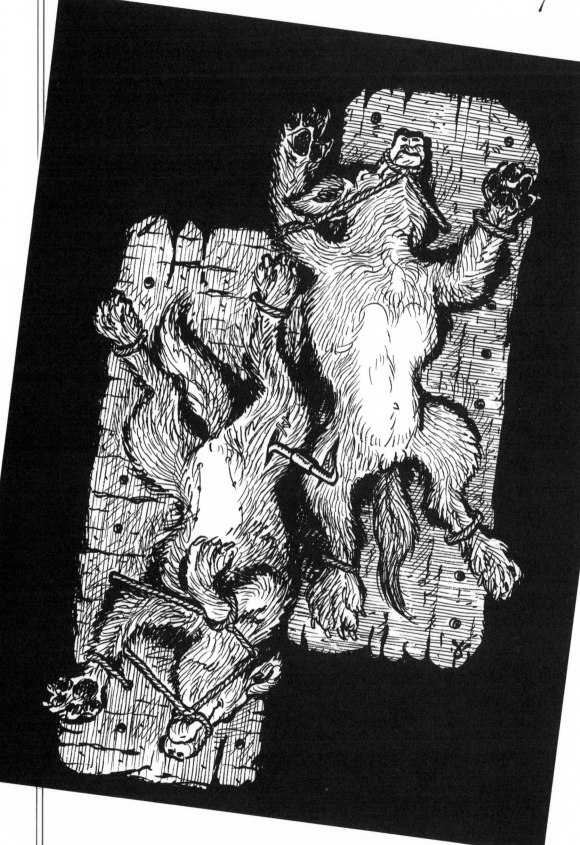

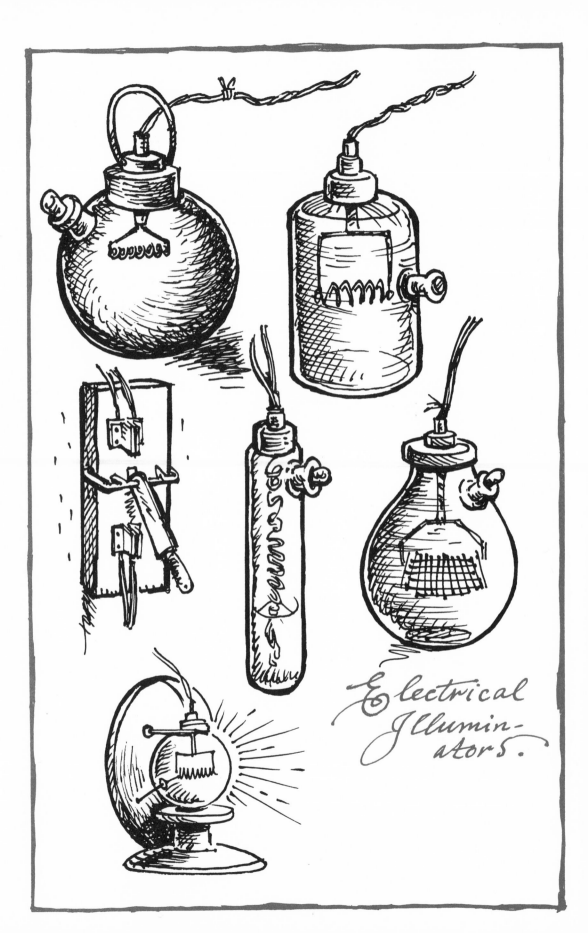

Electrical Illuminators.

Friday, 31 March 1815. — Rain.

The Late Springtime Rains prevailed this year. Last evening, during a particularly steady downpour, and whilst I worked late in the Laboratory, there came a heavy knocking on the front Portal.

Franz answered, then later returned with some startling news.

A Local Woodsman had discovered a Corpse in the Forest. There were no Missing Persons reported in the district, so he assumed that a passing Soldier became Lost and possibly was killed by Wolves.

The Woodsman, a rather inarticulate fellow, said that he would prefer not to venture this Late night down into the Village and wake the Constabulary. He thought that the Body might simply be interred on the outskirts of our Family Cemetary, which is located just within the Castle's Courtyard. For reasons other than those prescribed by the Woodsman, I agreed.

Franz departed with the Woodsman, then a short while later, Franz returned alone — with an unwieldly Burlap Sack.

I helped him lift the Bag to a low Bench, where we shook out the remains of what once, when assem-

1814 Spring.

EQUIPAGE FABRICATION LIST.
German Craftsmen & Tradespeople

✓ Der Zimmer - CARPENTER. Houses, Mill Drives, Water Wheels, Castle Repairs.

✓ Der Schreiner - WOOD JOINER. (Cabinet Maker), Furniture, Chests, Tables, Immersion Tanks, Laboratory Furnishings.

Der Wagner - WHEELWRIGHT. Wheels & Carriages.

Der Bütner - COOPER. Barrels, Tubs, Casks, Buckets.

Der Holzdrechßler - LATHE TURNER. Boxes, Cases, Bedposts.

✓ Der Gießer - FOUNDER. Cast Iron, Hardware, Cook Pots.

Der Schoßer - LOCKSMITH. Bolts, Chains, Grates & Iron Objects.

Der Papyrer - PARCHMENT MAKER. Sheep & Goat Skin - Ec.

✓ Der Glaßer - GLAZIER. Glassware, Blown Glass Retorts. Equip.

✓ Der Brillenmacher - SPECTACLES MAKER. Eyeglasses, Lenses, Metal Frames Leather, Horn, Tele & Micro Scopes.

Der Apotecter - PHARMACIST. Herbs, Purges, Prescriptions.

Der Balbier - BARBER-SURGEON. Salves for Wounds, Cures for Syphilis, Cataract Operations, Pulls Teeth, Cuts Hair & Bleeds Patients.

bled, was a Man! These grisly parts had clearly lain in the Woods for many Months.
The Arms and Legs were badly decomposed, the Torso was emptied of its soft Organ Contents — and the Skull was filled with Worms.

Although I had seen similar ghastly sights during my days and nights at the Charnal and Slaughter Houses, the smell of Death made me qualmish and I quickly turned away.
I left the room while Franz "fleshed" the Corpse, eliminating the traces of any extraneous matter unnecessary for our continued Study.

———————————————————

Tuesday, 25 April 1815. —

Corpse No. 2.
Specimen Acquisition.

Our second Corpse was acquired in a rather curious manner.
A Workman, who had been hired to re-channel a Mountain Stream for the Water-Wheel chute, discovered a crude Coffin buried just outside the Castle Walls.
Uncovered, it proved to be a complete, well-preserved Skeleton of a middle aged Woman. From all appearances, she seems to have been set to rest here about 10 to 15 years ago.

✓ Der Circtelschmidt - TOOLMAKER.
Compasses, Tongs, Pliers &
Craftsmen's Tools; Saws.
Electrical Apparatus.

✓ Der Meßerschmidt - CUTLER. Knives,
Scalpels & Scabbards.

✓ Der Kupfferschmidt - COPPERSMITH.
Pails, Basins, Troughs, Tubs,
Vats, Pans, Wine Bottles, Stills.

Der Nagler - NAIL MAKER. Nails,
Jacks & Wire.

✓ Der Dratzieber - WIRE DRAWER.
Copper, Brass & Iron Wire.
Twisted Wire, Covered Wires,
Wire Brushes, Musical Instru-
ment Strings.

✓ Der Bectschlager - BASINMAKER.
Brassware, Water & Electrical
Fixtures & Connectors.

Der Kandelgießer - PEWTERER. Molds
Flagons & Bottles, Keys, Platters,
Pitchers, Candlesticks etc.

Der Wägleinmacher - SCALES MAKER.
Balances for Weighing.

✓ Der Laternmacher - Lanterns & Boxes.

✓ Der Sieber - SIEVE MAKER. Flour
Sifters, Spice & Herb Scrapers.

Der Hefftelmacher - PINMAKER.
Smoothe, Round-Headed Pins of
Brass Wire & Clothes Clasps.

With vain promises of a proper
Holy interment, once again Franz
accepted this Corpse with our
Experiment in mind. This Skeleton took its place in our
fast-growing Museum of
Scientific Curiosities.

Friday, 5 May 1815. — Corpse No. 3.

The third Corpse arrived within
days of the last, by a completely
different means. A Local
Highwayman-Bandit named
Black-Jack Birenbaum was
captured and held for trial.

There was little doubt of the
Thief's guilt and Black Jack
was summarily condemned to
death and hanged by the Neck
at dawn upon the Gibbet, on
the outskirts of Town.

A cold seasonal Storm drove
the handful of Bystanders
quickly back to the warmth
of their Homes.

As fortune would have it, during
a particularly torrential moment
of the Storm, Franz and I
passed the Place of hanging on
our return to the Castle.

✓ Der Hafner - POTTER. Clay (mixed with hair) for: Jars, Pots.
Der Tiles; Glazed, Painted & Fired.
Der Spiegler - MIRROR MAKER. Frames & Magnifying Mirrors.

✓ Der Zeigler - BRICKMAKER. Smoothe Bricks, Rooftiles, Furnaces.

✓ Der Gürtler - BELTMAKER. Leather Drive Belts, Harnesses.

✓ Der Thatcher - BASKETMAKER. Weaver of Willow & Straw Baskets.

Der Seyler - ROPEMAKER. Heavy Ropes for Ship Hoisting Materials, Snares & Nets. Ropes & Cords.

✓ Der Bergtnapp - MINER. Ores, Minerals, Salts, Crude Oil, Coal, Salt.

✓ Alcohol, Charcoal; Phosphors; Salts Chlorine, HCl., KCy, Charcoal, Inks; Pens & Graphite Pencils; Paper / Furnaces, Cogs, Tables, Vats, Casks, Funnels, Filters / Brass Screws, Tubing (Flexible & Solid.)

Hurriedly, he climbed the Noose-Post and cut-down the Corpse. It fell into our Chaise and we quickly exited the scene.

Due to the foul weather, our Workmen's labors were also curtailed. Thus, there were no witnesses when we hauled this intact Corpse into our Laboratory.

Jack was a ponderous Man, and we struggled under his dead weight.

_____

Monday, 26 June 1815. — Corpse № 3.

This Cadaver appears to be in somewhat better condition, permitting a more thorough examination.

_____

Tuesday, 15 August 1815.

The first enthusiasm of success hastens me onward. Life and Death now appear to be boundaries which I may cross. If I should create a new Species, it would bless me as its Creator; no Father could claim the gratitude of his Child so completely, as I should deserve that of my own Creatures.

Castle Frankenstein
on Rhine
22 September, 1815.

My Dearest Elizabeth,

I am living in the abandoned Watch Tower of the Family's Castle, located close to the Town of Goldstadt. At Night the Winds howl through our Quarters despite makeshift Repairs. Only Franz is here to help me with my Scientific Work.

I am on the verge of completing an important Experiment. You must have Faith in me my sweet Elizabeth.

I pray that You will continue to wait. For now my Work comes first, even before you.

All my Love,

Victor. F.

Saturday, August 19 1815.

I believe that if I can bestow
Animation upon Lifeless Matter
I might, in time (though I
now find the notion un-attainable),
be able to renew Life after Death
has devoted the Body to its deeds.

I hope that to which I have dedi-
cated myself is justifiable; how
many Months have I dabbled
among the unhallowed damps
of the Grave, or tortured Living
Animal to animate the lifeless
Clay?

———————————

September 1815. — Quest for the Spirit.

Considering the great Advances
in the Art of Medicine during
this last century, I wonder why
so little attention has been payed
to the Science of the Human Mind?
Do we not all experience at some
time deep Melancholy, Hysteria,
pains of Passion and other Maladies
of the Nerves? But there is
little relief for the Psyche —
except from the Opiates, or from
strong drink.

I believe there is a Process for
"Healing a deranged Mind."
With the help of appropriate
Medicine, or through Discourse,
or Laughter, as propose by

There are no entries in Frankenstein's journal for several months, during which Frankenstein suffered a mental, physical, emotional, and even spiritual breakdown.

Nearly two months passed as Victor lay in a state of near catatonia. In his dementia he called out for his beloved fiancée, Elizabeth, who was far away in Switzerland. His faithful servant Franz took care of him.

While recuperating, Victor became even more preoccupied with the "process of life." His journals and notes reflect Frankenstein's growing obsession.

Dr. Boerhaäve of Leyden and Dr. John Brown of Edinburgh, one might find respite from one's own Psyche.

And I wonder, what shall be the Psyche of One who is snatched from the Grave and given Life again?

Sunday, 22 October 1815. — Corpse Nº. 3.

My limbs tremble, but then a restless, and almost frantic, impulse urges me forward; I seem to have lost all soul but for this one pursuit.

Also, it appears that our seemingly "unorthodox Scientific Practices" have caused considerable talk in the Village. And, despite confidences, the knowledge that I receive illegal Corpses and the Remains of dead Animals has spread throughout the Village, damaging my reputation.

Our work should move toward a speedy conclusion to avoid any unexpected remonstrations.

Franz now tells me that the local Constabulary has come by to make enquiries about...

IV

The Creature

Frankenstein's Human Life
Rejuvenation Experiments

Apparatus

20 January 1816. — Weather: Cold.

Once again I take up my Pen to set forth the details of my Scientific Explorations. Months passed while I suffered Mental Delusions which clouded my rationale.

This time now past, health has returned. I am again invigorated by prospects of the successful conclusion which lies close within my grasp. Having reviewed my Notes after severade months of inactivity, I find that I am within days of my anticipated goal. Now, I truly possess the capacity of bestowing Anima-tion to the Human Frame.

Tuesday, 1 February 1816. — Corpse N.º 3.

I set out to prepare this Human Cadaver, with all its Fibers, Muscles and Veins in place — a task of inconceivable difficulty and labour. It is now ready to receive the Vital Energy.

I had long doubted whether I should attempt the Creation of a Being, but my imagination was too Stimulated by earlier successes to permit any further doubt.

Monthly Budget:

1. Lease on Castle from Land Graffe
   Hesse, Royal Land lord.
   Plus: Annual Property Taxes.
   = 5 Ducats.

2. Wages for 4 Part-Time Employees.
   Plus Salary for Franz.
   = 6 Florins

3. Purchase of Diligence, including
   Saddlery & Bridalry for 2 Horses.
   = 3 Thalers .12 K

4. Payment for Castle's Repair and
   Remodeling - = 1 Ducat.

5. Basic Furnishings, Tables, Chairs,
   Utensils, Beds & Blankets.
   = 6 Ducats.

6. Materials, Equipment & Services.
   Necessary to conduct my work.
   = 5 Ducats.

7. Day-to-day Living Expenses.
   = 10 Florins.

Dr. Frankenstein's total basic monthly expenditures equals to about $1,000. 1990   U. S. Dollars.

The Materials to accomplish my work are now within my command. The Cadaver is adequately preserved from spoilage through an ingenious arrangement of Franz's clever devise.

Wednesday, 31 April 1816. — A Cold Spring.

It has been Spring for over six weeks and still the skies are black and the snow falls brown upon the already thick ice.

The Sunsets, on days when the Sun shows itself, are often Spectacular!

Sunday, 4 August 1816. — 4 Months have passed since last entry.

Winter, Spring and Summer have passed while I labored; I am deeply engrossed in my Ghoulish Occupation.

My Enthusiasm is checked by my anxiety; I am like one doomed to toil and slave in the mines, or any other unpleasant trade, rather than occupied as an Artist with his favorite employment.

Every Night, I am beset by a slow Fever; I shun my fellow man as though I were an Outcast. It is only my Scientific Purpose which sustains my energy.

I believe that some small exercise and amusement would drive away this incipient disease, and I have promised to reward myself with these pass-times once my Creation is completed.

Sunday, 3 November 1816. — Apparatus Prepared.

Our objective is now within sight. With Franz's assistance, nearly all the Apparatus is working as designed, and the Electrical Equipment promises to be even more effective than imagined.

Monday, 4 November 1816. — Very Cold.

The Weather has turned extremely cold. The earliest stages of Winter appear to be upon us. The water bucket froze last evening.

Strangely, Franz has become more difficult to understand. Although his enthusiasm for our work remains, his concern bespeaks more of his impending return to home and family in Krakow.

Sadly, upon opening the Frigeration Cabinet which preserved the Cadaver, we discovered that despite all our precautions, too much time has passed and it has turned to a stinking pile of jellied flesh. Franz mercifully buried the near-liquid Remains away from the Castle as I attempt to fumigate the Laboratory with burnt Balsam and Rose Water.

The Lever. ✳ *Reflectors* ✳ *Examinatio*

5 November 1816.   — Cadaver № 5 !

Suddenly, a turn of good Fortune.
Most amazingly, a New
Cadaver - № 5. - Quite fresh, and
by far in better condition than
our previous Anatomical
Corpses - has been secured secretly
from a local Inn-Keeper. Franz
tells me that it is the Body of
a Farmer from a nearby province,
aged about 35.

It was said that about a year or so
hence, while this Farmer was in his
fields, his Wife was violated, then
murdered by a band of passing
Soldiers.   The Farmer's two young
Children were also put to the Sword.
Upon his return to the House, he
discovered their lifeless bodies and
went insane. He abandoned his
Farm - its Crops and Livestock -
and all these Months has sojourned,
like a Wild-Man, throughout the
Mountain District, frightening the
country Citizens.

98.

Several Days ago this Mad-Farmer, it was said, terrorized a local Tavern, and late the previous Night, he was discovered rifling the Inn's stores for Food.

The land lord accosted him, and struck him fatally in the Head with a Shovel. Then, to avoid any Police investigation of his deed, the Inn-Keeper hastily made the Corpse available, at no Cost, to Franz and myself.

9:00 PM. —

— My Work Begins.

<u>Wednesday, 6 November 1816.</u>

On this dreary night in November I behold the accomplishment of my toils. With an anxiety which almost amounts to agony, I have collected the Instruments of Life around me, that I might infuse a Spark of being into the lifeless Thing that lays at my Feet.

With a silent prayer to the Creator of the Universe, I begin my fearsome work. All is ready — Franz and I have tested every piece of Equipment, every Item of Apparatus and the Electrical Mechanisms.

All the Tools have been arranged on Tables and each polished, ready to perform its Special duty. Static-

Electricity, which we've generated within the Laboratory, crackles in the air and an Electrical Storm approaches from the North.

Cadaver No. 5. has proven the best of the lot. Due to the extreme cold his Flesh shows little signs of deComposition. Franz has washed-down the Body and I have attempted to close up some deep Cuts in his flesh. Especially problematic is the deep and probably fatal Gash to his Frontal Cranium. This I have secured with sutures.

A Special Note: Upon administering a minute Electrical Charge, Cadaver No. 5 appears in death to have possessed a tiny Flutter of Breath, and the inside of his Thighs remain Warm.

With all due respect to this Corpse, I will not open his Chest for autopsy. The most Severe damage to this Cadaver (No. 5.) is mostly on his Cranium.

Blood from many of No. 5's wounds has "congealed," but perhaps there is sufficient amount of this Vital Fluid to re-vivify the Creature?

I performed a Transfusion of Blood from my own arm, then opened No. 5's Skull by Cap removal. I released the pressurized Fluid within the Skull. Next I conducted an Examination of the Head Wound, which dis-

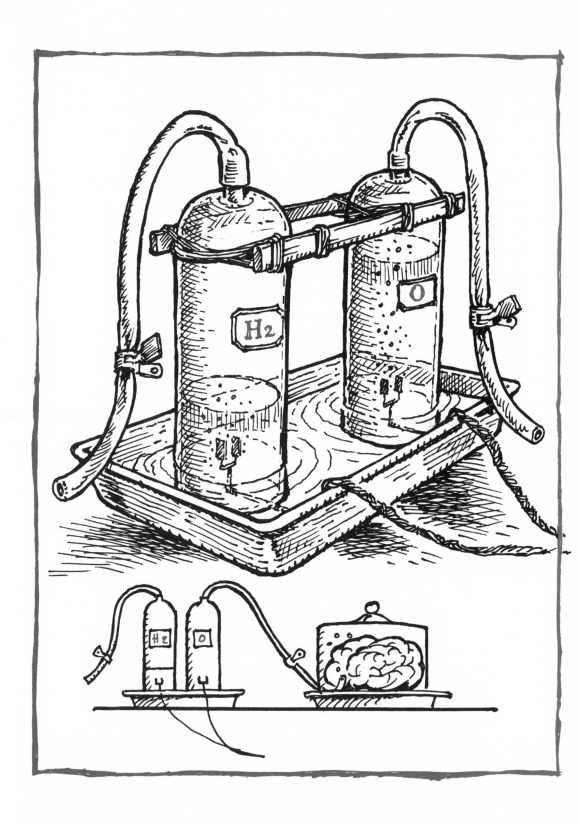

closed only minimal damage to the inferior Cerebrum. The Brain is intact. I accidentally discovered that by stimulating various segments of the Brain with small Electrical Probing Devices, I was able to elicit Movement from various parts of the Creature's (№. 5.) Anatomy – Hands, Face, Arms, Legs.

I replaced the Skull-Cap, and attached the Hair with small Metal Fasteners and Silver Bone Screws, to keep its Skull Contents in place.

11:05 P.M. – Storm, Wind-Rising Fiercely.

Wednesday, 6 November 1816.

APPLICATION OF RESPIRATION DEVICE.

After cleansing and repair, and with Franz's assistance, we quickly moved Cadaver №. 5 to a Work Table near the Respiration & Electro-Cardio Stimulator.

Especially remarkable is the flexibility of the Corpse's Limbs and the Suppleness of his Skin. Also the process of RigorMortis appears not to have set in, due possibly to its general "freshness" or else from the recent and extreme coldness which the Cadaver № 5. has sustained.

Despite a few flaws in our Equipment, we have attached a MECHANICAL RESPIRATION DEVICE – which stimulates Cadaver № 5's Auto. Breathing Processes, in hopes of restoring his Blood-Oxygen / Nitrogen gasses.

106.

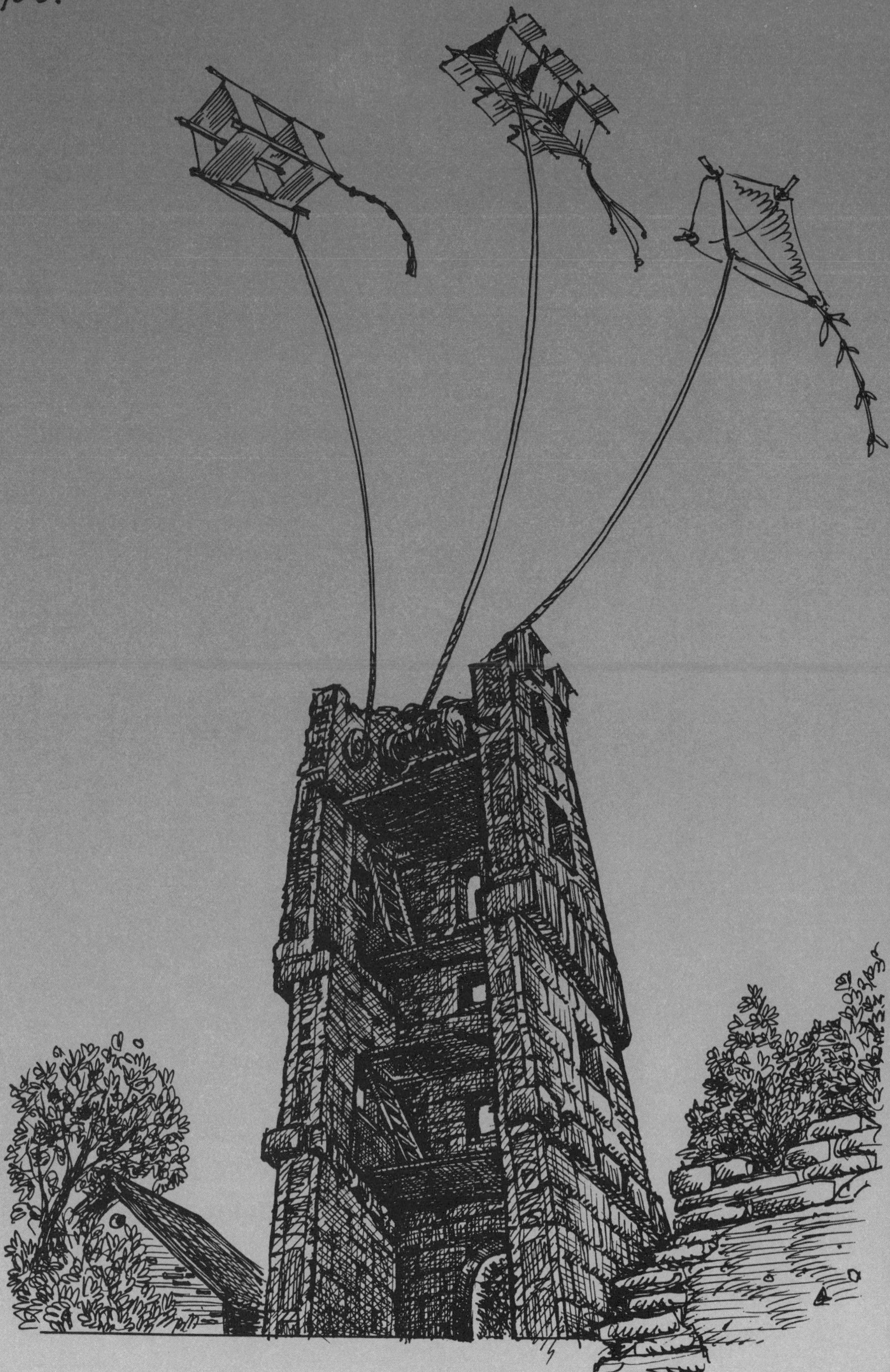

Also, by our employing an efficiently functioning Hydro-Oxy Electronic Gas Separation System, a pure supply of Oxygen (& N.) is now being pumped directly into N° 5's un-used Lungs.

___

Nov. 7. – MIDNIGHT. – Storm full upon us.

As per previously arranged, and with hopes of sustaining and containing all Electrical Energy, Frank and I installed a Series of Leyden Jars in which we hope to collect Electricity. These Jars will be filled with Electrical Life Energy as it passes through the Copper Wires from the Electro-Generator Devices. We will also gather Electricity by a Series of Silk Franklin-Kites, which we've hastily launched from the Castle's Tower Roof in expectation of the fast-approaching Electrical Storm.

___

12:40 AM. – Storm begins, ushered by Near-distant Lightning, Thunder.

Thursday, 7 November 1816.

N° 5's HEMO-BLOOD SYSTEM:

Upon examining N° 5's Blood System, I attempted a Transfusion of Lamb's Blood directly into his Veins, this in hopes to supplement his apparent loss of Sanguine Fluids due to his unseemly violent and Bloody Death. It's most difficult to discern

Nº 5's Temperament, though from reports it might be, as expected, Fiery Choleric.

The Human Heart is more complex than any other Organ in the Human Body; and its function as the seat of Man's Soul is only paralleled by its action as a Fluid Pump to the whole System.

Nº 5's Heart must be Electrically Stimulated into activity as soon as possible.

2:00 AM.   – The Storm.

Thursday, 7 November 1816.

Amazingly, the elements necessary for the great Experiment are all in place. Tonight's Electrical Storm has arrived at an ideal time; Cadaver Nº 5 came into our possession in near-excellent condition and at precisely the correct moment in Time; and after these years of scientific planning – of trial and error, gain and loss – these next moments may indeed brush the cheek of God.

The Creature, Nº 5, is hoisted up by the windlass, which suspends it above the galvanic Saline Immersion Tub. Even now, the Laboratory crackles with Electrical Sparks, which leap from Leaden Wires from the Kites which Franz guides into the Storm Clouds outside on the Roof.

"Pops" and Explosions spray the room. Power and Electrical Energy churns and buzzes as it collects within the Leyden Jars. All of the Laboratory Apparatus begins to Glow. My equipment comes alive with Light!

I increase the Saline Solution to the Blood, and No. 5 responds when Electrical Current is applied.

The Creature bubbles furiously with Electrical Heat like some Archaic Cauldron, aboil with the Potion of Life.

I administer Oxygen through a Facial Cup.

The Cardiac Rheostat derives Power from an Alternating Electro-Static Generator, which sends a stream of Variable Energy to the Creature's Chest and Heart.

Electro-Stimulation of the Heart sends Vital Fluid through dormant Veins, and (I pray) will re-vivify this Lifeless Creature.

The Creature is immersed in the Galvanic Bath. The Oxy-Respirator and Cardiac Rheostat Systems are continually employed.

Thirty minutes after the stimulation, the Creature was lifted out of the Galvanic Immersion Tub.

The Rheostat is detached while Oxy-Respiration continues..

THE CREATURE BREATHES! HIS HEART BEATS! HE MOVES!

HE IS ALIVE!

3:30 AM —

Thursday, 7 November 1816.

The creature LIVES!

Franz and I removed the Creature from its Apparatus-Table and prepared Him for his first Examination.

The Creature has been transferred to the Examination Table, Electrodes detached, Limbs and Extremities stimulated, Brandy administered through the Mouth - Nº. 5 is covered with Blankets.

4:00 AM.   Nº 5.

PRELIMINARY EXAMINATION:

Cranium: — Irises: Contracted / Marked
              Sclaractasia!
       — Considerable Ostial-dermia
              in the Frontal Region.
       — Exterior Electrodes:
              Inducted Vital
       Energy into the Body.

Blood: — Pressure:
       Systolic — Over 300!
       Diastolic — Over 200!
       THREE TIMES NORMAL !!
       — Definite Hyper Pituitary,
       — Minus 65 ?!
       That accounts for his Great
       Size!

Heart: — Heartbeat: 250 beats per
              minute.
       No Human Heart could
       possibly function at this
       rate! He's completely
       Super Human!
       — Left Ventricular Propond-
       erance ... There are
       TWO Bullets in his Heart!

Micro: — Poly-Morphal Cellular
              Blood...
       — Extreme Hemocrosis.
       — The Alpha Lucascites
       apparently don't dissolve?

Microscopic:
       The Entire Structure of
the Blood is quite different from
Normal Blood. The Cells seem to
be battling one-another — as if they
had... a life of their OWN !

RESULTS OF EXTERNAL EXAMINATION:

The Creature was aparently brought to Life by an Electrical Impulse of Terrifying Potency! Specifically: AN EXTRACT FROM LIGHTNING! — Some Super Violet Ray, far beyond the known Electrical Spectrum!!

SUCCESS! The Creature is ALIVE!

Movement Response registered in his Hands, Eyes, Face, Mouth!

The Storm is spent! Night passes wretchedly. I sink to the ground through languour and extreme weakness. The excitement of my success is coupled with the horror, bitterness and disappointment of my work having become manifest, and that my Dream may now become Hell to me!

Early A.M. — Dark, Cold Steady Rain.
Thursday. 7 November 1816.

Morning already. Rain patters dismally against the window panes. All is dim as my candles are nearly burnt-out. Franz has crumpled exhausted on a nearby pile of grain sacks — by the glimmer of a half-extinguished light, I see the dull Yellow Eye of the Creature - OPEN!

The SECRET of LIFE & DEATH

Matter ages because it loses Energy!
This Artificial Body I have
created has been charged with
Super-Human Power, so that its
Span of Life will be extended.
It's Lifetime will equal the Lives
of more than a hundred Human
Beings... This, my CREATION,
can never perish unless its
Energies are drained   Artific-
ially, by changing the (Electrode)
Poles   from   PLUS (+)
          to   MINUS (−).

Energy which cannot be destroyed
          CAN be Transmitted!

Connecting the PLUS (+) Poles to
the MINUS (−), will CHARGE
the Energy output to the System.
As by connecting the   MINUS
(−) to the MINUS (−)... will DIS-CHARGE?

It breathes hard!

— and a convulsion suddenly agitates
its once flaccid limbs
— Is this a Dream?

His Features are beautiful!
great god! His grey-blue Skin
seems to scarcely cover the work
of Muscles and Arteries beneath.
His Hair is lustrous black and
long-flowing; his Teeth of pearl
whiteness, his Nails a dangerous dark blue! These luxuriances
only form a more horrid con-
trast against his watery yellow
Eyes, which seem almost the same
color as the dun white Sockets
in which they are set. His shriv-
eled Complexion and straight
black Lips are only distinguished
by the fresh red Scar, cut deep
down across his Forehead, Cause
of his Death; struck by a Shovel.

I worked nearly two years for
the sole purpose of infusing Life
into inanimate Bodies. And
finally here before me is THIS
for which I have deprived
myself of all health & relaxation.

_____

— Cold,
Driving Rain.

1816 — AM. Thursday 7, November.

Again, I awoke from a wild and
disturbing Dream in which I
embraced my beloved Elizabeth.
I dreamed, as we kissed, that her

Lips took on the livid hue of Death, and her features changed — until this Dream dissolved to my holding the Corpse of my dear dead Mother in my Arms, Her Funeral Shroud enveloped her delicate Form as it crawled with Grave-Worms in the folds of its Flannel.

—The Rain Ceases, Storm Clouds blow through...

(Written Later): 9. am.

The end of this dream was of Lightning. Fireworks and Colorful Sky-Rockets — only to realize it is Some last random Flash from last nights evening Storm. I Started from my ing sleep with horror! — A cold dew. Sweat covered my Forehead; my Teeth used as chattered, and every Limb convulsed, with a Palsy. I even have great diffic-ulty using this Pen, and must warm my-self against the Candle. Illness and fatigue have struck me down into a fitless sleep last Night upon a pile of Wet Straw on my Laboratory Floor.

(Written Later) — 2 PM?

The yellow Light of the Moon shone through the Clouds and a high Stained-Glass Window: and again I beheld the wretched and miserable Monster whom I have created.

— He Moved!! —

... He sat upright, then pushed aside the Bed-Curtains. And his Eyes were fixed intently upon Me. His Jaws opened and He muttered some inarticulate Sounds as a troubled Grin wrinkled across his Cheeks. Then, he stood, and stretched out one of his Hands as if to detain me. Was this a Nightmare or was it real?

I escaped and rushed down Stairs, then outside to take refuge in the Castle's Courtyard, where I remained for the rest of the night. I recall walking around in an agitated State. I listened attentively, fearing every Sound, as if it were the approach of the Demon Corpse to which I had given Life.

Franz was nowhere to be seen — He's most assuredly fled!

When I gazed upon Him unfinished, He was ugly, but now that his Joints, Muscles and Limbs are rendered capable of motion, He is a "Hellish Thing" that even Dante could not have conceived!

Friday, 8 November 1816. — Rain.

Outside, the weather is dismal and wet. The morning has at last dawned! To my Sleepless and aching Eyes, this Sunless day began at the sixth-hour, at which

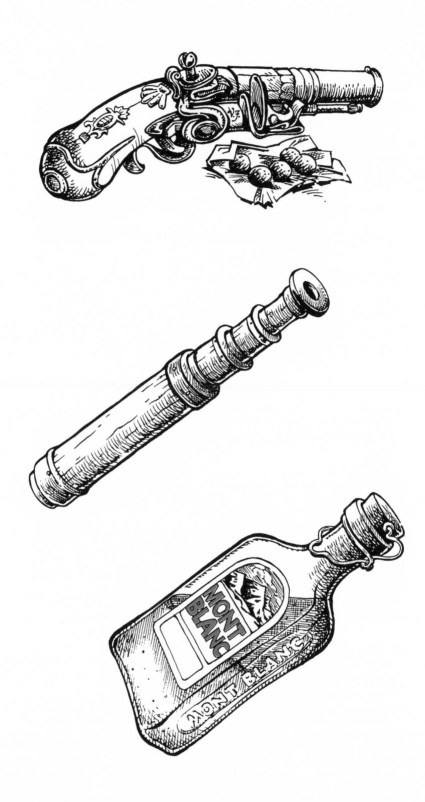

point I opened the Castle Gate, passed out of the Courtyard and issued into the fog-shrouded mountain Road and Forests beyond.

Although drenched by a Rain pouring from the black and comfortless Sky, I dared not return to my Laboratory where I left the horrible Wretch.

Hours passed. At Noon, or later, I found myself wandering the muddy and rock-strewn Hillside Roadway near the Village.

Suddenly, I observed a Swiss Diligence which paused in its journey to stop just where I was standing. The Door opened — and I beheld my dearest friend Henry Clerval.

As we made our way back up to the Castle, Henry asked many questions, and answered others I had of my Father, Brothers and Sweetheart Elizabeth.

"They are uneasy," he replied. "They hear from you so seldomly."

On seeing Clerval, memories returned of my home so dear. For the first time in months — for a moment — I forgot my misfortune. Henry remarked how very ill I appeared. I knew this to be true, and confessed my deep preoccupation with my work.

Clerval and I arrived back at the Castle. I dreaded to behold again that Monster whom I had left in my Laboratory so many hours before, but I feared still more that my friend Henry should see Him.

Gone too was Franz. Had he guided The Creature somewhere into hiding? Would they both, or each, come bursting into the Room at any moment? Or, did they both finally abandon me?

While I was gone, the Servant, Magda, arrived. Unaware of the previous night's events, she brought in a breakfast of Tea for Clerval and myself. When asked the whereabouts of Franz, she only shrugged her Shoulders. I became convinced that he'd chosen to leave my Service. Concerned and disappointed at his untimely resignation, I knew of his wish to return to his Home and Family.

Henry was concerned about my erratic behavior. I laughed and cried wildly and un-restrained – then finally Confessed my Crime.

I felt myself slip away into a state of despair.

123.

<u>March - April 1817.</u> — Many Months have passed.

My health, under the steward-ship of Clerval, has returned. Weeks passed. I began to feel stronger, and as the seasons changed, my hope was renewed.

Then, Grief once again arrived at my doorstep.

One cool afternoon, shortly after the Spring thaw, some local Men arrived to tell us they'd found Franz. His strangled, broken and naked Body was discovered not far from the Castle, secreted beneath the forest's leaves. Rumors claimed he'd been seen dragged there, weeks earlier, by a huge rough Giant.

Pain and dread renewed within me.

<u>1817 - Summer - Autumn.</u> — Months Later.

Many Months have passed since my Illness. Plans are set to close The Castle Frankenstein. My friend Clerval is assisting me. By now, from my fevered rantings, Henry is aware of my deeds.

My Secret is safe, but we wish to keep it from other prying Eyes. There was no word of the CREATURE and no trace at all of his where-abouts.

124.

1817 - 1818. Winter. — Health Returns.

Eventually, my Mental Sickness and Melancholia abated enough for me to travel with Clerval to my Father's home in Geneva, where my Family and my beloved Cousin, Elizabeth, all awaited my return.

1818. Spring-May. — Spring Renewal.

A Celebration of Springtime was held in the Village. The Peasants were dancing and everyone was gay. Henry suggested that we attend, and while there bid our farewells to the Citizens of Goldstadt. My Spirits were high, and I bounded along with renewed feelings of anticipated joy.

On our return to the Castle, I found a letter from my Father. In the letter he disclosed that my youngest Brother — Little William, was Dead!

That sweet Child, whose Smiles delighted and warmed our Hearts, had been Murdered! The details rushed through my mind like water over a Spill-way. My Family had gone for a late Spring Afternoon's walk. At Dusk, as they prepared to return to the House, William was no longer with the Party. They searched the Woods, then returned late that night with Torches.

But, William was lost! At Dawn his little Body was discovered on the damp forest grass, with marks from the Murderer's Fingers still upon his fragile white Throat.

When the news reached my Elizabeth, she fainted! When she awoke she wept unconsolably. Only that very afternoon, she had let him wear her Miniature Portrait Locket of my beloved Mother. And now the Picture Brooch was gone! doubt- less, temptation for the Deed. I wept bitterly, then hastened to Clerval, insisting that we return instantly to Geneva, and to order the Horses at once!

After days of travel and hardship, we drew near to the familiar environs of Geneva. It was dark, the Town Gates were shut and a Storm was approaching rapidly from the north west. I had resolved to see the place where brother William was murdered.

The Plainpalais was lit by Lightning which danced across the Mountain Summits.

Arriving at the Spot I watched the Tempest, so beautiful yet so Terrific! I clasped my Hands, and exclaimed aloud: "William, Dear Angel! This din Is thy Funeral Dirge!"

The following account of events and the Monster's own story have been pieced together from the few remaining entries in Victor's journal and the bundle of letters found in the trunk.

To everyone's surprise, a close family friend, the maid, Justine Moritz, was accused of William Frankenstein's murder.

Circumstantial evidence, the discovery of little William's portrait-locket in her possession, forced a conviction. Her trial was to be held in a few days, so Victor and his family visited her in jail. There, she was confused and continued to blame herself for the death of her small friend.

At the trial, the family spoke in Justine's favor, and Victor, knowing her true innocence, pleaded valiantly for her sake. But Justine's confused manner only mired her deeper into guilt. Her forced confession sealed her fate.

Despite the family's protest to the judges, Justine was condemned to death and was hanged the following morning.

The House of Frankenstein went into mourning. Victor shut himself away in his rooms, or alone went sailing on the lake. He often wept bitterly and openly.

Victor ventured upon several local journeys. He wandered the Alpine trails, visited ruined castles, and climbed Mont Blanc.

One day, while scaling the Great Glacier, he sought shelter from a seasonal rain beneath a rocky protrusion. He beheld the figure of a man, who quickly came upon him.

It was the Monster. Victor trembled with rage and horror as it approached him. He cursed the Monster for his hideous murders—then he cursed himself for having created this Devil.

Suddenly, in the gloom, behind some trees - I beheld a Figure. I stood fixed, gazing intently; I could not be mistaken! A Flash of lightning illuminated the Scene, and It's gigantic Stature was revealed.

The Deformed Shape was more Hideous than I recalled. It was the Filthy Demon, to whom I had given Life!

I Shuddered! ~~HE~~ was my brother's Murderer.

Two years had elapsed Since that Night when He first received Life. Was this his virgin Crime? Or was poor Franz his first victim?

I Created a depraved Monster whose delight was Carnage and Death!

I kept vigil on the Spot, and eventually the Storm and the Wretched Monster faded into the Dawn.

About 5 in the Morning, I arrived at my Father's House and requested the Servants not disturb the Family.

As I walked through the Home which I had not Seen for over Six years, all passed as a Dream.

As best as I can, I have tried to reconstruct the Creature's story in an impartial and distanced voice, untainted by the feelings surging through me as I listened to words which took me through a frightening range of emotions from pride at his learning and self-suffiency to blood-chilling hatred at his unspeakable deeds.—V.F.

The Creature's Tale

The Creature told of his own wretched existence; of the hatred he had endured for every minute of his being. And now, for him to experience detestation from his Creator—this was a punishment too unjust and too great to endure.

Now, face to face with his Creator in a hidden mountain cave, the Creature sought answers to questions that plagued his mind since that first instant of consciousness.

He said he barely recalled his first moments. He told how strange sensations seized him; all was darkness and silence, then light and sound poured in. He sought food, water, refuge, and then he lay down in the woods, overcome by sleep.

When he awoke, it was dark and cold and he felt pain at the cold and sat up and wept. Looking up, he saw the stars and the moon and wondered at their beauty. He noticed the sounds made by little winged creatures and wondered at their origins. He felt compelled to articulate what he was sensing around him and frightened himself by the uncouth sounds that emerged from his mouth.

As he stayed on in the forest, he began to learn to differentiate the various creatures and plants by their shapes or sounds. He became accustomed to the pattern of light then darkness then light that seemed endlessly and reassuringly to recur.

He discovered a fire left by some people and, delighted by the warmth it created, reached into it with his hands, only to withdraw them in immense pain. By trial and error he learned to tend the fire from a safe distance and keep it alive with twigs and branches; he cherished it as his source of warmth and light.

After sleeping for several hours, he awoke and, driven by curiosity about this new place which was not the forest, walked toward what seemed to be a cluster of huts in the distance. He walked through the village, and was drawn to the neat, attractive dwellings with colorful flowers in window boxes. He stopped at a house with colorful trim, opened the door and entered. The children inside saw him first and began to cry; then their father, wielding an andiron, swung wildly at the large and frightening intruder, driving him into the street. The neighbors, now roused by the commotion, grabbed sticks, stones, anything that was at hand, and all together chased the Monster from the village, all the while shouting curses and threats.

He escaped from the village, retreating to the countryside, where he came upon a rustic cottage which had beside it a storage shed which had fallen into disuse. He went inside and made a decision to make it his home, a welcome escape from the elements and from the barbarity of mankind.

He made himself a straw bed and slept close to the wall so he could feel the warmth of the fireplace, which was on the other side of the wall. He took bread and water from the owners of the cottage when they were away.

Food was scarce and only a few roots and nuts were found to ease his hunger. He was consumed by a drive to find sustenance; so much so that he left his fire and went out in search of food or human beings who would be able to provide it. After wandering through the woods for three days, he finally came upon an open field. He felt relief when he saw a small thatched hut in the distance, for it had snowed the night before and he was freezing cold and hungrier than he had ever been.

He approached the hut; the door was open, so he entered. A man was inside and he was preparing some food for his morning meal. When the man saw the Creature, he shrieked in fear and ran from the hut. The Creature devoured the food that had been prepared, then lay down on the straw hut in the corner and fell asleep.

Through a chink in the wall that the cottage and shed shared, the Creature watched and listened to the occupants. They seemed unhappy in spite of the fact that they had food and shelter. As he watched some more, he began to realize that the room was quite small for three people—the old man, who appeared unable to see, the young man and the girl. He saw that they had little to eat, he watched the young man toil in the fields from morning to night, and he watched the girl labor at household tasks all day long.

One evening, eager to ease their distress, he took the young man's tools and went into the woods, returning with a vast amount of firewood—four or five times as much as the young man could cut and transport in a full day. When the family discovered it, they were astounded and full of smiles and hoots of joy. The Creature watched in satisfaction from his hiding place.

He listened and learned their names—*father, sister, brother, son*, and the names they gave to the familiar objects in the cottage—*fire, milk, bread, wood*. He learned other words that appeared to describe things that weren't objects at all but things which came from inside them—*happy, unhappy, good, bad, hungry, full*.

He stayed the whole winter hidden away in the shed, watching his family and learning their language. When Spring came, a beautiful dark-haired woman of a people they called Arabic came to live with the son. She too had to learn the language and the son read to her and to the creature, hidden away on the other side of the wall, from the only book they had, Volney's *Ruins of Empires*, and through its pages he learned a basic knowledge of history and gained some insight into manners, governments, religion, as well as of virtue and chivalry, of kings and decline.

He learned of property, rank, descent, nobility, classes, peasants, and slaves. He listened to see if he could learn of what category he was a part. He learned he had no property, no rank; he was not even a slave, bound in servitude to another. He was alone and there were no others like him. As his ignorance and innocence were replaced by knowledge and understanding, his inner pain intensified. He felt only his Creator would have answers to heal his anguish.

The Creature continued his tale, telling of the journey to find his Creator, which next led him to the Jura Mountains and a doomed encounter with a lovely boy child. He said the child came running to him fearlessly, full of curiosity but with none of the alarm that grown men had shown in his presence. The Creature was seized by a desire to educate the child as his companion and friend so he would not be lonely anymore. As he reached out toward the boy, grabbing his arm to bring him closer, the child screamed out "Let me go! Let me go, or I'll tell my Papa. He's Victor Frankenstein and he'll punish you."

The Creature, welling with hatred at the mention of his Creator's name and also in fear of being discovered, closed his hands on the throat of the child to stop his screams. Before the Creature realized the harm he was inflicting, the child slumped over dead, his locket, chain broken, dangling sadly from the Creature's hand. In a panic, the Creature ran looking for a hiding place. He came upon a barn and entered to find a young woman sleeping there and gently, not to disturb her, hid the locket amidst the folds of her skirt. Little did the Creature know he took two lives that day, as the hapless young woman, Justine Moritz, would later be executed for the child's murder . . .

By the glow of the fire in the cave, the Creature's voice rang out, a rational man making a reasoned demand of an equal. "You must make a woman for me, a woman like me. I am alone and miserable upon this earth and I must have a partner to help me endure this wretched life you have given me, a partner who is as deformed as I without and with the same intensity of feeling within. I swear by the sun and by the blue sky that if you grant my wish of a Bride, we will depart together and you will never behold us again."

V

The Bride

Frankenstein Creates the Creature's Mate

134.

1818   The Autumn.   —   My Father's Home in Switzerland.

I am resolved to dedicate myself to this most abhorrent task ahead. I cannot attempt to compose a Female Creature without devoting many months of profound Study & Labour.

I had heard of certain Scientific Discoveries made by a former University Professor of mine from Ingolstadt: a Dr. Praetorius, who now lives in England. His findings are based on New Principles, which I believe to be material to my Success. Concealing the true reason for my venture, I hoped to obtain my Father's consent to travel to England and Scotland, to meet with the Professor.

My Health has been restored, although my Spirits darken with blackness each time I consider my unpleasant promise to The Creature.

Father is concerned at my seeming lack of affection for dear Elizabeth, and has pressed me to be honor-bound in my 'trothal.
But I can offer no reply. I must yet create the Monster's Mate! It is yet too soon for us to enjoy a peaceful and delightful marriage.

---

19 September 1818. — SWITZERLAND.

Thus, I have begun the last phase of my loathsome career with lengthy correspondences to Dr. Praetorius in England.

He encouraged my theories and offered his full assistance with my Project. — He invited me to Scotland to witness his work. In his facilities I could conduct my own scientific work uncontested.

The plan was thus: Clerval and I would travel to England and Scotland, where I would remain for several months on the pretense of studying with Dr. Praetorius. Henry would return to Switzerland.

In truth, I would, with the Professor's assistance, create yet another Monster! This time — a FEMALE!

Wednesday, 23 September 1818.

The Crates and Boxes packed for my Voyage also contained many of the Chemicals, Apparatus and Instruments I shall require at our final destination. My family and Elizabeth bade me a fearful but silent farewell, and I began my Journey.

1818 - October to November. — SWITZERLAND TO EN ROUTE.

Henry and I travelled through Europe toward England. Our tour first took us to Strasbourg, then up the Rhine River to Mannheim, where we passed many ruined Castles. Once again we arrived at the village of Goldstadt near the Family Castle, but stayed only overnight at the Inn.

The following morning, as we glided along our route down stream, I was depressed. The travels were pleasant — the cloudless blue sky, Nature's tranquility - but I dreaded the work that lay ahead.

Beyond Cologne, we descended to the plains of Holland, and arrived in a few days at Rotterdam. By Sea, we crossed the French Channel to England. Henry grew anxious with our progress.

Sunday, 27 December 1818   TRAVEL
                          HOLIDAY SEASON

After a short sea voyage,
I saw the white Cliffs of Dover
Britain. Soon after, we Sailed along
the Banks of the River Thames.
The Steeple of London's St. Paul's,
and the city's infamous Tower-
Prison were all in view.

We remained in London for nearly
a year to see the Sights of the
great City, then Henry remained
behind as I continued my
travels.

_____

Wednesday, 22 September 1819. — Scotland.

Today I visited my University
Professor, Doctor Praetorius. He
was one of School's strangest
Characters. Admittedly, I had
only a dim memory of him as, during
my first year, he'd mysteriously
failed to return to his Classes
after a holiday. Rumours prevailed
that Praetorius had been found
performing "Un-natural" Experiments, and he hadn't been
heard from Since then.

Doctor Praetorius began with praise
of my Student days, and what he
believed were the parallels of our
professions. I little dreamed that
my association with him would com-
plicate my already burdened existence.

Over large quantities of Gin, he told me of his own Experiments in Creating _Life_. He'd grown Human Cultures from his own Human Seeds!

Then, Praetorius, like some slurry Parent, Showed me the Hideous Fruits of his filthy labour.

Tiny, twisted Human-like Beings, a few inches high, floated, turning lifeless, pickled in Laboratory Jars of Alcohol. Their yellow Eyes gazed sightlessly upon us as we talked.

Next, the Professor settled upon the true purpose of our meeting; he too wished to create a Living Creature — A MONSTER!

I suspected that My Monster had followed me to Scotland, and that He would reveal himself when I delivered to him his Female Companion.

The Professor and I planned to travel farther North to the remote Orkney Islands. There we could conduct our labors.

1819 - 1820 Winter. — The Orkney Islands.

What madness has brought me here? For many months we have lived upon a great Rock in the Sea, five miles off the Mainland. The ocean continually beats on the bleak

Cliffs. The barren soil, which scarcely affords pasture for the few miserable cows and goats, is as gaunt and contemptible as the Island's Inhabitants. The whole Island has but three decomposing Huts; the one which I have hired contains two squalid Rooms. The Thatch has fallen in, the Walls are unplastered, and its Door is off the Hinges.

These were repaired, and our Laboratory was erected. We proceeded in our labours, which became more horrible and irksome daily. It was indeed a filthy process in which we were engaged.

During our first Experiment, an enthusiastic Frenzy blinded me to the horror of our proceedings; my mind was fixed intently upon our all-consuming Labours.

1820, Nearly Spring — The Orkney Isles.

The Sun set and the Moon rose out of the sea. I have lost all track of time — and have only some vague sense of Seasonal Change.

Only three years ago, I was first engaged in the creation of a murderous Fiend! Now, I am about to form a female Monster — a MATE for this barbaric Beast!

But — might this "Bride" be ten thousand times more malignant than her Mate? And, would he fulfill his oath to quit the places of Man and hide in the deserts? Would She comply?

Only when this female Monster is complete will the Consequences be disclosed. Might He abhor the sight of her female Form? Will She turn from him with disgust, and then both threaten the species of Man?!?

15 March 1820. — ORKNEY ISLE LABORATORY.

She arrived only two days ago. The Professor and I lifted her from the Row Boat and carried her slender, lifeless body up here to the House.

Now Praetorius celebrates with his gin, interspersed with whiffs of Nitrous-Oxide gas and quantities of Laudanum. He entreats me to join him.
Instead of Celebration, I perform the examination of this "Bride-to-be," preparing her body for <u>Life</u>.

Female Cadaver. No. 1.

Age: 16 - 17 ?
Height: 5'5"
Weight: Approx. 8½ Stone
Dark Hair.
Blue Eyes.

General Health in Life: good

Cause of Death: Strangulation with rope.

It was apparent that the Girl had been Strangled. Our task, providing we are Successful, is to embue Her Corpse with the Spark of Super Electrical Ray-Power. Our past experiences have proven this will increase Her Physical Strength — a hundred fold!

This Corpse had delicate Hands and Feet. This Girl, with the freshness of childhood still on her cheeks, was just the age of my Elizabeth when we first betrothed. The tender Flesh of her slender Throat and Neck are Scarred raw by the Strangling Garrote Rope, still pressed tightly upon her windpipe.

Why would this harmless girl be murdered?

Then the terrible Answer!

With ultimate Beastiality - evidence of her Rape - and murder as her payment! Not even my Monster would be capable of such a viscious dishonor -

This Flower must be reserved only for Mortal Men of Human Society.

I immersed Female Cadaver Nº 1. in a Saline Tank

All the while, I sensed the forboding presence of His great dark Form.

I know He is near - waiting.

_____

16, March 1820. — ORKNEY ISLES LABORATORY.

I saw the Dæmon through the Casement. He was lighted by the Moon. A ghastly Grin wrinkled his thin black lips. He had followed me in my travels, then loitered in the forests, hiding him-self in caves, taking refuge in deserted heaths. Now he comes to mark the progress of my promise. I locked the door in fright, and vowed never to resume my hideous Labours. My last thoughts were of exhaus-ted sleep on my rude Bed.

I was awakened several hours later by the sound of voices in the adjoining Room. Leaping up,

I stumbled out to find my associate, the drunken Professor Praetorius, sitting casually at table in the dim candle-light, quaffing a pleasant vintage Madeira with My MONSTER!!

He turned my way and raised his goblet, "Oh? Victor! I've been having a most enlightened conversation with your charming friend. I've assured him that our goal is imminently in sight, and if he simply relaxes for a few hours, I've promised him a surprise."

Praetorius rose and came to me, then whispered that he'd drugged the Creature's cup, and that our large guest would soon retire.

Within moments, the giant stood, then staggered like a wounded Elk, crumpling to the floor in a drunken heap.

"Well, doctor? Shall we begin?" Smiled Praetorius.

I salvaged many of my most important Scientific Implements and Apparatus from the Castle; and though they had been stored for nearly three years, I brought only the Equipment most easily adapted to our present needs.

Quickly, we attached an Electronic Apparatus: The Breathing & Respiration Mechanisms and the Blood Pumps to the FEMALE.

Female Cadaver Nº 1's body had not been frozen, as had her male predecessor — and now the hardness of Death and her Tissue deterioration had already well begun.

I next attempted a hasty Blood Transfusion to pump fresh Fluid into her system. No young Animal was handy, so I transfused my own Vital Body Fluids. Her veins barely received the Needle

Praetorius scurried about the place, he engaged the Drive Wheels, manipulated the Static Electricity Generators, adjusted the Equipment Mechanisms and filled the many Leyden Jars with Precious Life-giving Electronic Fluids.

The Female Creature was lowered into the Saline Galvanic Bath. Rheostatic Control was switched on to its lowest Power. The first Stimulating Electronic Sensations were sent into the Dead girl's lifeless Body.

After more than 70 Minutes of Electrical Stimulation, there was little reaction from the Cadaver:

Muscle Reflexes: - UN-RESPONSIVE.
Eyes & Pupils: - MILKY-DILATED.

Blood Transfusion: UNSUCCESSFUL.
Blood Pressure: NEGLIGIBLE
                BARELY: 5 over 2
Respiration: - UN-REFLEXIVE.
Pulse: 0 : 0 = SHE WAS WITHOUT
                     ANY LIFE.!

For over an hour I was overcome by the Sensation of helplessness, almost as in a frightful dream. I wished to fly from this impending danger - but I was rooted to the Spot.

Laughing insanely, Dr. Praetorius danced about the Electrical Apparatus, swilling Gin from his bottle and babbling Poetry. Why was he so joyful when our Experiment had been a failure?

Suddenly, I heard footsteps, and the door behind me opened.

The wretched Monster appeared, prepared to claim his Bride. Praetorius danced up to meet the Creature, embraced him fatherly, and offered his Bottle of Spirits. The Beast brushed aside the frail Professor and, through his yellow Eyes, surveyed the Scene.

The Monster moved slowly across the floor toward me.

The Creature Spoke: "You have destroyed the Woman! What do you intend, Frankenstein? Do you break your promise to make a Wife for me!?"

"Begone! you Wretch! Yes! Yes! I do break my promise, and never will I create another deformed and wicked Monster such as yourself!" I Screamed!

Meanwhile, Praetorius had gone un-noticed to the Female Corpse.

He appeared to be working over her.
The Monster gnashed his teeth
and spoke to me once again:
"As each Creature on this Earth
has its Mate — I too have feelings
and emotions, Frank-en-Stein.
Why should I alone live with only
detestation and Scorn?"

Praetorius called to us.

The Monster and I both turned.

The Professor, in his gleeful drunk-
eness, had trussed-up the Female
Monster in a bizarre Bridal
Costume of bed-sheets and had
placed Some Scattered Island Flora
in her hair. He stepped aside,
then bowed a deep gesture of welcome
to this grotesque Mannikin.

"Behold!" he boomed. "The Bride,
Creature of Dr. Frankenstein!"
What was disclosed beneath the drape
made me turn away in horror!
The once youthful Girl was now
a gray, discolored Corpse. She
now stood upright-strapped by
leather restraining Belts to a
make-Shift wooden Tilt-Table.
Her flaccid and decaying Limbs
Strained and Sagged against gravity,
as a putrid yellow Oil Spilled
from her body Cavities and
oozed across the filthy Flag-
Stone Floor.

The Monster came at me again.
"Whilst I live with this wretch-
ed-ness, you dare to des-troy my

Mate.   Re-venge re-mains.
Be-ware, Vic-tor Frank-en-
stein! You pass-ion-less Souls!
My ve-nom runs deep, and I will
tor-ment you. I will go now, but
re-mem-ber. I shall be with
you on your wed-ding night!'"

The Monster moved to the door,
then observed once more the mockery
of his prospective Mate. He Snar-
led at the dead Girl's hideous Form,
then angrily pushed over a Lantern
nearby, which fell and burst
into flames.

I rushed back to drag the drunken
Praetorius from the fire as the
Monster fled without a second glance!

In moments the whole house was
aflame. I managed to drag the
Professor to Safety, but retrieved
only a few belongings, including
my Journal.

We escaped into the darkness.

17 March, 1820. — DAYLIGHT, ORKNEY
                        STONE BEACH.

The following day there was no trace
of either the Monster or the
Professor. I returned to the burnt
Hut's Stone Shell, and sorted through
the ashes. Only the Bones and
Scraps of that pitiful Girl
remained, which I gathered together in a Basket for burial
at Sea.   I had resolved never
to undertake these atrocious
Creations again!

VI

The Return

Frankenstein's Fate

152

17 March, 1820. — NIGHT, AT SEA.

Anxious to leave this place, as planned, I set-off to join Henry Clerval in London for our return to Geneva.

I placed my meager possessions aboard the skiff, and as the Moon arose this night, I sailed toward the Scottish Mainland.

About 4 miles from shore, when the Moon disappeared behind a cloud, I cast my basket and its grisly contents into the sea. I listened to the gurgling sound as the Bones of this girl sank to the deep, then I sailed away from this spot.

18 March, 1820. — DAWN, SEASIDE VILLAGE.

After a considerable long voyage to the Mainland, I finally arrived at the shore of a small fishing village. I landed at the Harbour, and whilest fixing the Boat and arranging its Sails, was surprised to be Surrounded by a Small Crowd of People. They offered me no assistance, but whispered and gestured toward me. Their language was unlike any I'd heard, neither Scottish nor English. I was most inhospitably received, then taken to see a Mr. Kerwin, the town's Magistrate.

Mr. Kerwin, who did speak my native language, asked me to give an account of my actions for the last night. A gentleman had been found dead, and I was the only stranger to visit the village. Startled at this news, I knew that my innocence could be easily proved.

— Constabulary Quarters.

Several Witnesses arrived and said they had discovered a gentleman dead upon the beach early the night before. Initially, they believed he'd drowned and washed ashore - but his Clothes were dry and his body was still warm. Upon examination, they described him as a handsome young man, about five & twenty years - he appeared to have been strangled. The Murderer left bruised finger marks upon his throat.

Witnesses had seen a Strange Boat with a Single man Shortly

before discovering the Dead Man's body. Several hours later my boat was observed in the vicinity.

Mr Kerwin took me to another room where the victim's Body lay so that they might observe the effect it would have upon me.

As I looked into the Coffin, I gasped for Breath! and like a Nightmare — I saw the life-less form of Henry Clerval stretched before me! ——

Clerval. My Friend, My Benefactor!

I could not sustain the grief, and was carried from the room convulsing (So I was told later).

I was taken to the gaol's Dungeon where Several days later, during my recovery, Mr. Kirwin entered to provide Some consolation for my misfortune. In my possessions he'd discovered several Letters from my Father. Kerwin quickly dispatched a letter to Geneva and having recently received a reply — told me that someone, a Friend, was coming to visit.

I thought of poor Clerval, and of his Hellish demise. I shouted in agony to "Take him away! Do not let him enter!"

assuming the Creature had returned
to further torment me — My
Father entered the Cell and
all my fears dissolved.

Father calmed me with pleasant
news of Brother Ernest and my
beloved Elizabeth. He only
dwelt on interests of my Heart
to raise my Spirits.

We weren't permitted to converse at
any length, and shortly thereafter
Mr. Kerwin entered to usher
my Father out.

June 1820. — PRISON.

After three months in Prison,
the Assizes finally arrived to a
nearby town. I was forced to
travel there, while Mr. Kerwin
arranged my defense. My case
was not even brought before
the Court. The grand Jury rejected the Bill because I proved
I had been on the Orkney Islands
at the hour Clerval's
body was found. A fortnight
later, I was liberated from
Prison. But I cared little for
freedom; whether a Dungeon
or a Palace, the Walls were
hatefully alike to me.

Father and, I took passage aboard a Vessel bound for Havre-de-Grace, and Sailed with a fair wind from the Irish shores.

I lay on the deck looking at the stars and listening to the waves; my pulse beat fast as I reviewed my whole life. I Shuddered with Sadness and wept bitterly.

August 1820. — SHIPBOARD & BY LAND TO PARIS.

From he Havre, we Sailed on to Paris, where we paused to rest before once again continuing our journey. My Father's care was indefatigable; but not Knowing the origins of my Sufferings, his remedies were all for naught.

— A few days before we left Paris I received a Letter from Elizabeth.

My dear Friend,

It gave me the greatest pleasure to receive your letter dated from Paris. You are no longer at such a formidable distance, and I may hope to see you in less than a fortnight.

My poor Cousin, how much you have suffered. This Winter has passed most miserably, as I too have been tortured with suspense

I know that many misfortunes weigh upon you.

I dare not prolong in writing what I'd dare not the courage to express before. You know well, Victor, that our union had been planned by our Parents since our infancy, and we were told to look foreward to this event, even as affectionate playmates in Childhood.

As children, we often entertained a lively affection to each other, but never did we desire a more "intimate" union — a mutual happiness.

Please answer me, dear Victor — do you not love another?

I confess that when I saw you last Autumn, unhappily flying from me into solitude, I could only suppose you regretted our Connection.

I confess to you, my friend, that I love you — and that in my dreams, you are my constant friend and companion.

Do not let this letter disturb you, my friend: and do not answer if it gives you pain.

But, when you return, if I see but one smile on your lips when we meet, I shall need no other happiness.

Your Loving,

Elizabeth
La Vena

Geneva, August 18, 1820.

1820, 6 September. — TRAVELLING THROUGH FRANCE, GENEVA.

Father and I continued our journey across France to Switzerland; and after about a week we arrived home at Geneva.

Sweet Elizabeth welcomed me with warm affection, yet there were tears in her eyes as she beheld my feverish and emaciated frame. She too had lost much of her vivacity, though her gentle compassion comforted me.

15 September 1820. — GENEVA.

The short-lived tranquility found upon my arrival at home did not endure. I remembered The Monster's vow: "to be with me on my wedding night!" and a fury possessed me.

Only Elizabeth had the power to draw me from these fits; her gentle voice soothed and inspired me.

Soon after our arrival home to Geneva, Father spoke of my marriage to Elizabeth. I remained silent, and thought of the Hellish intentions my Fiendish Adversary had planned.

But Preparations for the Marriage were made, and congratulatory visits received.

Part of Elizabeth's inheritance had been restored by the Austrian government, and it was agreed that immediately after the Wedding we would spend our first days at Villa Lavenza, which overlooked a beautiful mountain lake.

In the mean time, I took every precaution to defend my person, in case the Fiend should openly attack. I carried two pistols and a Dagger! Indeed, as our Wedding Day drew nearer, The Monster's threat appeared more a delusion, and the happiness which I hoped for in my marriage now seemed more certain than ever.

20 September 1820. — MARRIAGE.

On our Wedding Day, Elizabeth was melancholly. Perhaps she thought of the dreadful secret I'd promised to reveal to her on the following day.

My Father was overjoyed during the bustle of preparation.

The ceremony went well, and afterward a large party was assembled at Father's house.

Father presented Elizabeth and me with the Traditional Orange Blossom Bouquets and Boutonnière. He said they had been passed along by Father to Son over the last three Generations of Frankenstein marriages.

Despite the festivities, I continued to feel apprehensive. The whole Village turned out for for our Wedding Celebration and the Mayor himself officiated.

In the midst of our Celebration, M. Dowpreeth, the town's Wood-Cutter, Shocked the Village when he brought his freshly murdered Daughter, Maria, into the Town Square. The Killer was said to be a Strange and Gigantic Monster! I knew it could only be my Hideous Creature, who followed me again, all the way from Scotland!

_____

September 1820. — ALONG THE RIVER.

All Smiled upon our Nuptial Embarkation. As Elizabeth and I commenced our Wedding Journey by water, our first night would be spent at an Inn at Evian. The next day, our Sailing winds were again favorable.

Those were the last moments of my life during which I enjoyed any remote feeling of happiness. We passed rapidly along the rivers, shaded from the hot Sun, and enjoyed the scenic beauty.

Elizabeth entreated me to "Be happy, as there is nothing to distress us." She assured me that she was indeed content. Thus Elizabeth endeavored to divert our thoughts from any Melancholy Subjects.

The Wind, which had hitherto carried us along, diminished rapidly at Sun Set to a Slight breeze. I guided the Boat to Shore, and as we landed, my fears were revived.

The Water, Woods and Mountains were obscured by the darkness as we made our way toward the lights of the Inn.

Once there, we retired to our Suite of Rooms. A Sudden Rain Storm began.

A thousand fears arose again in my mind. Anxious, I grasped the Pistol hidden in my bosom. Silently, Elizabeth observed my agitation, and trembling She asked what I feared.

I replied for her to remain at Peace, and that after this dreadful night all would be Safe. Then I earnestly entreated her to retire to her rooms.

I hoped to obtain Some knowledge as to the Situation of my Enemy. She departed.

I passed the hours inspecting the hallways and corners of the Chalet. But I found no trace of the Fiend, and hoped that Some fortunate Chance had intervened to prevent this menace.

Suddenly! I heard a fearful Scream from Elizabeth's room! I rushed into her Chamber.

There She lay thrown across the bed, her Head hanging down, pale and distorted; Her Face half-covered by her Hair! For a moment I lost my Senses and fell to the floor!

When I recovered, I was Surrounded by other horrified Occupants of the Inn. Scrambling to my feet I ran back to the room where my Love, my Wife, my Elizabeth lay <u>dead</u>.

She had been moved, and now lay properly upon the bed. A Handkerchief covered her Face and Throat.

I rushed forward and embraced her with ardour, but the coldness of her limbs indicated that she had ceased to be the beautiful Elizabeth I cherished and loved.

Looking out the Window at the pale yellow Moonlight, I saw the most hideous Figure! The Monster jeered, pointing his fiendish finger at the Corpse of my Wife ——

I rushed to the Window, drew my Pistol — and FIRED! but he eluded me, running swiftly away and plunging into the Lake.

The Pistol's report brought a Crowd into the room, and Search Parties were immediately organized and dispatched into the Woods.

I attempted to accompany them, but a short distance from the Inn, my Head whirled and I fell into an overwhelming state of exhaustion! I was carried back to my room and placed into Bed.

Later, I awoke and crawled to the room where the Corpse of my Beloved lay. There were women weeping there — and I joined my sad tears with theirs.

I knew not whether my only remaining friends were safe from that Maligned Fiend. I then resolved to return to Geneva with all possible speed.

September 1820. — GENEVA.

When he learned of the events preceding my return, my poor Father grew despondent. Within a few days he was unable to rise from his bed. He eventually died in my arms.

? October 1820. — PRISON.

I awoke in a dungeon with recollection of things past.

The Melancholy or madness which led me to a Solitary Cell, was now followed by a clear picture of my situation.

Upon my release I repaired to a Criminal Judge, and accused the one who destroyed my family. The Magistrate listened attentively but as I unveiled the details of my narrative, I sensed his surprise mingled with disbelief.

The Judge replied that he would be willing to aid in my pursuit, but wondered who could follow

Such a Creature, one that could traverse the Sea of Ice, and inhabit hidden Caves and Dens. I broke from his house, frust-rated and near insane!

— TRAVELING.

October and November 1820.

After these events I quit my beloved Geneva and my home Country. With a sum of money, together with a few jewels, my wanderings began.

I traversed vast portions of the Earth, endured hardships of Climate, weather and Barbarous People. How I lived, I hardly know. Many times I fell upon my knees, and prayed for Death to free me. But revenge kept me alive! I dared not to die — and to leave my Adversary unpunished!

I called upon the Spirits of the Dead, and on the wandering Ministers of Vengeance to help me conduct my work.

Let the Cursed Monster drink deep of agony; let him feel the despair that now torments me!

Suddenly! I was answered by a loud and fiendish laugh which broke the stillness of Night.

As the ringing laughter faded, a familiar voice addressed me in a barely audible whisper —

"I am Sat-is-fied, Frank-en-stein, you mis-er-able wretch. You have de-termin-ed to live — and I am Sat-is-fied!"

Instantly, I ran to the spot from whence the voice came, but the Devil had once again eluded me.

— TRAVELING.

December and January. 1820-1821

Thus I pursued The Monster for many months, followed him along the winding rivers, until I reached the blue Mediter-ranean where I saw the Fiend hide himself within a vessel bound for the Black Sea.

I took passage on the same ship — but somehow He escaped me.

I next followed His trail amidst the wilds of Tartary and Russia. Many Peasants, frightened by His horrid Apparition, informed me of His path.

As the Northern Snows descend-ed, I saw the print of His

huge feet in the white plains.
Cold, wanting and fatigued,
I was destined to follow this
Devil; I lived in an eternal
Hell.

My Life passed, following the Monster. Only in Sleep could I
cast off the miseries of my
days to feel the joy I once knew
so long ago. In this sleep I
saw my beloved Country and
my benevolent Father; I
heard the silver tones of my
Elizabeth's voice, and beheld
Clerval enjoying health and
youth.

As I journeyed further North,
the snows thickened, and the
temperature dropped to degrees
too severe to bear.

Springtime 1821. — THE FROZEN
NORTH.

I have procured a sledge and
Dogs in which I traverse the
snow at a previously inconceivable speed. In a few short
days I gained on the Creature.

Invigourated by His spiteful
words, I resolved not to
fail in my purpose.

With renewed courage, I pressed
on and in two days arrived at

a Sea-Shore hamlet. The Ocean,
Covered with Ice, was distinguished from land by its barren,
rugged Surface. The Inhabitants told of a gigantic
Monster, whom they forced
to flee with guns.

May? / June? / July? 1821.
Had He escaped me? I exchan-
ged my Land-Sledge for an

— Ice Sled and a Stock of Provisions and set out with my Dogs
across the frozen Ocean.

Many weeks have passed. Driven
by rage and despair, I toiled onward until I reached the
Summit of an Ice Mountain —
— I viewed the expanse.

Suddenly! a Dark Speck
caught my eye upon the Icy
Plains. Was He now in
Sight?

There was no time for delay.
I fed my dogs as we rested for
a short time, then I continued
toward the Mystery Figure.
I perceptibly gained on it,
beholding my Enemy at
no more than a mile's distance.

My Foe was almost in my grasp.
but my hopes were
suddenly extinguished; a thunder
was heard, followed by rolling
Waters which swelled be-
neath me. I pressed on. —

The wind rose and the Sea roared.
With a shock not unlike that
of an Earthquake, the ice split,
and the Sea rolled between me
and my Enemy. I was left
adrift on a Chunk of Ice
that with time melted, and
grew continually smaller. I
feared a most hideous
watery Death!

Many hours passed, several of
my Dogs died; and as I was
about to Sink under the accum-
ulation of extreme distress, I
saw a Vessel riding at anchor.

I immediately disassembled my
sled to construct Oars;
I moved my Ice Raft closer
to the Ship. I'd hoped they'd
grant me a Boat to continue
pursuit of My Enemy.

But when I was taken aboard,
I became totally exhausted. Oh,
won't my guiding Spirit conduct
me to The Demon, allowing
me the rest I so desire; or
must I die — and yet he lives?!

"'Fate has cast me here upon this Nordic ice-floe. The realization that these may be my last moments upon Earth inspires me to justify, or perhaps elucidate, my actions.

If ever this Manuscript finds its way into Sympathetic hands, I pray that you, Dear Reader, be temperate with your judgement. My purpose was not, as may believed, an attempt to equal the phenomenon of our Divine Creator.

The goals of this quest were, instead, to further my personal knowledge of The Secrets of Nature - and to set own Notations for those who may come after me.

I sought to discover a Universal Panacea, with which to alleviate a Wife's childbirth pain, a Medicine to soothe that Babe from its anguish in days of famine and pestilence. I sought an Elixir to stave away the ravages of age - and if I may be forgiven - I did also Seek out the Holy Process whereby the Dead may be brought back, and Made to Live once again.

Scientific Procedure was the method I employed. The All-Knowing Creator of the Universe devised his

System for Man to unravel. Is it not then Man's purpose to attempt to emulate his Creator in all things virtuous

— Why then, should a quest for the Creator's most Arcane Secrets of healing and rejuvenation be avoided?

"That I succeeded, upon several occasions, in accomplishing these Miracles of Life Re-Vivification, may never be believed, though herein (within this book) are my Procedure.

I struggled often with the impossibility of my chosen task, although now there remains little evidence of my success, only this Slim Journal and perhaps the lingering memory of the Creature whose existence is dismissed as only Legend.

I ask, Dear Reader, that you exonerate me for what may seem, in these days of darkness, as blasphemies of a cluttered and troubled madness.

Begging the Creator's mercy and forgiveness.

Dr. Victor Frankenstein

— the North Sea, 1821.

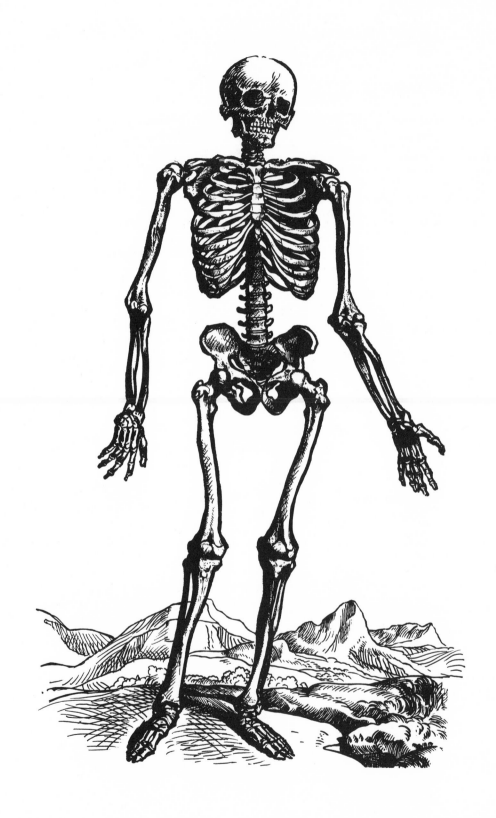